treaty shirts

gerald vizenor

TREATY SHIRTS

October 2034 — A Familiar Treatise

on the White Earth Nation

Wesleyan University Press | Middletown, Connecticut

Wesleyan University Press

Middletown CT 06459

www.wesleyan.edu/wespress

© 2016 Gerald Vizenor

All rights reserved

Manufactured in the United States of America

Typeset in Sina

Hardcover ISBN: 978-0-8195-7628-6

Ebook ISBN: 978-0-8195-7629-3

Library of Congress Cataloging-in-Publication

Data available on request

5   4   3   2   1

IN MEMORY OF MY GRANDMOTHER

Alice Beaulieu Vizenor

AND MY FATHER

Clement William Vizenor

The ideal of a mode of government that mirrors the values of a single community is dangerous because it implies that plural identities are pathological and univocal identities normal.

John Gray, *Two Faces of Liberalism*

In America today our great divide in many ways comes down to a feud between the repressions of correctness, on the one hand, and freedom, on the other. Were correctness to prevail, its know-nothingism and repressiveness would surely lead to cultural decline. Even if freedom offers no guarantee of something better, it is at least freedom, and the possibilities are infinite.

Shelby Steele, *Shame*

A man of imagination has an advantage over other people, in that an actual experience is almost always less intense than his expectations of it. An actual misfortune is almost always less painful to him than his fear of it, just as, of course, his actual experience of joys is almost always less stirring than his hopes and anticipations of them.

Lion Feuchtwanger, *The Devil in France*

Finally there is a justice, though a very different kind of justice, in restoring freedom, which is the only imperishable value of history. Men are never really willing to die except for the sake of freedom: therefore they do not believe in dying completely.

Albert Camus, *The Rebel*

CONTENTS

treaty shirts

ARCHIVE

The Great Peace of Montréal became the mainstay of our visionary and catchy petition that autumn for the right of continental liberty. Seven native exiles resumed that singular treaty of peace in tribute to thousands of our native ancestors, the ancient voyageurs and coureurs de bois of the fur trade, and citizens of New France.

That theatrical peace treaty was plainly signed forever and has continued in native stories as a trustworthy entente after more than three centuries of diplomacy, territorial wars, colonial turnabouts, separatism and reservations, and the many obscure resolutions of sovereign nations.

Seven native exiles teased the former colonial regimes to restore that great peace of the continent and recognize a singular seat of egalitarian governance at Fort Saint Charles on Manidooke Minis, the island of native liberty, mercy, and spiritual discretion near the international border of Lake of the Woods.

Archive is my nickname, one of the seven exiles.

The Constitution of the White Earth Nation, once our chronicle of continental liberty, was created with moral imagination and a distinct sense of cultural sovereignty, the perseverance of native delegates, and a certified referendum of citizens, but the duties of our democratic government were carried out for only twenty years.

The rightfully elected government, related community councils, and judiciary were abandoned overnight when the original treaties and territorial boundaries of the White Earth Reservation were abrogated by congressional plenary power on October 22, 2034.

The exiles were sworn delegates to the constitutional conventions, and then with the defeasance of treaties and governance the seven exiled natives turned to the irony and tease of native stories, and a chance that the great union of peace would overturn in spirit the course of termination and native banishment.

The Constitution of the White Earth Nation would continue as an autonomous native government in exile, we resolved that autumn, with the recommenced ethos of the Great Peace of Montréal at Fort Saint Charles.

Native traditions were turned into kitschy scenes at casinos, the conceit of culture, vain drumbeats, and with a bumper cache of synthetic narcotics, but native stories, the rough ironies of our liberty, and creative starts and elusive closures, outlasted the treachery, clandestine chemistry, the empire warrants, and the monopoly politics of entitlements.

Natives have forever escaped from the treachery of federal treaties, ran away to adventures, love, war, work, and money, broke away from reservation corruption, but we were the first political exiles with a constitution. Liberty has never been an easy beat, tease, or story.

The seven exiles and a native soprano in her nineties were steadfast that any history must be envisioned with native stories, and our ancestors were rightly saluted, an easy gesture to more than two thousand native envoys who gathered three centuries ago on the Saint Lawrence River near Montréal and entrusted forty orators and chiefs to sign by name and totemic mark the great peace union with the royal province of New France.

Justice Molly Crèche, one of the native exiles of liberty, naturally praised the sentiments and native signatories of that historic peace treaty, the first colonial empire to honor native sovereignty and continental liberty. She declared that native stories were survivance and diplomatic trickery, and our petitions to continue that peace treaty entailed ironic reversals of the colonial cession to Great Britain in the Treaty of Paris.

La Grande Paix de Montréal has never been abrogated in tact or forsaken in diplomacy. Yet, that historical union and memorable peace treaty was directly connected to the decimation of totemic animals in the empire fur trade and has never been forgiven in the court of shamans, or revised with irony in the native stories of colonial enterprise and the shakedown of liberty.

Come closer, listen to the steady crack of totemic bones, trace the bloody shadows and getaways, endure the steady wingbeats of scavengers, and count out loud the seasons and centuries of peltry stacked in canoes, the gory native trade and underfur treasure of two empires, and the everlasting agony of the beaver.

The beaver and native totems were sacrificed once in the empires of the fur trade and orders of courtly fashions, and then totemic animals were converted into tawdry casino tokens, the new crave of peltry and games of chance.

The animals of cagey casino cultures were considered more as a nuisance and the sources of new diseases than the traditional inspiration of survivance totems and continental liberty.

Native storiers and artists portrayed the outrage and cruelties of cultural memory, and recounted in words and paint the ruins of native totems and haute couture of the fur trade, the fancy curtains, carpets, and maladies of casinos. Native creation stories were derived from totemic visions, and the course of our survivance must relate to that natural motion of continental liberty.

Hole in the Storm painted a series of grotesque casino gamers aboard a giant luxury yacht on Lake of the Woods. The cheeky triptych, *Casino Whalers on a Sea of Sovereignty,* portrayed the great waves, backwash, and bloated gamers hunched over rows of watery slot machines with beaver and totemic animals in place of the cherries, numbers, and bars on the reels of regulated chance.

Hole in the Storm was one of the seven exiles, and the nephew of Dogroy Beaulieu, the renowned native artist who was exiled almost twenty years earlier for his shrouds of totemic creatures and scenes of decrepit casino gamers.

The White Foxy Casino commissioned seven original paintings by Auguste Gérard Beaulieu, or Hole in the Storm, a painterly native nickname, and at the same time casino curators organized an atonement exhibition to celebrate the distinctive and once traduced portrayals of his great-uncle Dogroy Beaulieu.

Douglas Roy Beaulieu, a visionary artist, created a sense of native presence and abstract portrayals of animals, birds, and totemic unions of creatures. His avian shrouds were acquired by museums around the world. Yet, the revered painter was menaced by the tradition fascists and banished from the reservation because of the portrayals he created of casino gamers connected to oxygen ports on slot machines, and because of his evocative images of totemic visions. The miraculous traces of natural motion, the spirits and shadows of dead animals and birds were revealed on linen burial shrouds.

The Midewin Messengers, a scary circle of blood count connivers, coerced several native legislators to disregard the specific article in the Constitution of the White Earth Nation that clearly prohibited banishment. The political ouster was reversed several years later, but the abuse and disrespect of a great native artist could not be undone with a customary tease, turnabout gossip, casino drumbeats, or generous waves of cedar smoke.

Dogroy actually thrived as an artist in exile, and, with the mongrel healer, Breathy Jones, earned a prominence he could not have achieved in the crude casino culture on the Pale of the White Earth Nation.

Dogroy connected with other painters and established the marvelous Gallery of Irony Dogs in the abandoned First Church of Christ, Scientist located near Elliot Park and the historic Band Box Diner, a distinctive native quarter in Minneapolis. Some fifteen years later a heroic bronze statue of the militant poseur Clyde Bellecourt was erected on the corner near the Gallery of Irony Dogs.

The best native trickster stories were teases of creation, traditions, marvelous contradictions, and ironic enticements of weird and visionary flight. The stories were never about the abstract patois of treaties, entente cordiale, or native sovereignty. Now our stories must tease and controvert the capitol promises and betrayals as much as the sex, creation, and hardy escapades of lusty tricksters. Some stories were risky, erotic hyperbole, and with no sense of shame because the sex conversions, masturbation, and other seductive adventures started with our ancestors. Candor was natural and the fakery of literary denouement was not necessary.

Newcomers, fur traders, missionaries, and the course accountants of reservation enlightenment seldom weathered the teases or survived the mighty twists of trickster mercy. Truly, the new sector governor deserved no greater standing in native stories than federal agents of the past century.

The United States Congress abrogated more than three hundred native treaties in a special session that Sunday, October 22, 2034, and at once substituted federal sectors for reservations and state counties to manage the burdens of social security and hundreds of other national strategies, entitlements, and endorsements.

The Congress considered but could not enact more reasonable measures to decrease the enormous national cost of covenants and entitlements, so the political outcome was only promissory, a compromise that ended native treaties, the entente cordiale of native sovereignty, and, at the same time, the legislators voted to commence with the national endorsement sectors.

Congressional plenary politics once more downplayed and then abrogated as a mere compromise native egalitarian governance, continental liberty, and cultural sovereignty. The national political cuts, causes, and economic enactments were never more than the revels of dominion and monopoly agencies, and the remnants of treaty reservations were at most the caretaker remains of deceptive sovereignty.

The poses of entente cordiale and native sovereignty were bureaucratic ruses, and yet some weary natives were encouraged, other natives, storiers, literary artists, and painters, resisted the political maneuvers, and many others capitulated, once, twice, more, and then came the inevitable reversal, the plenary abrogation of our continental entente, treaties, and native liberty.

Godtwit Moon was nominated the sector governor straightaway and the very next day he posted an order to banish seven natives from the reservation and sector. The order indicated only our nicknames, Archive, Moby Dick, Savage Love, Gichi Noodin, Hole in the Storm, Waasese, and Justice Molly Crèche.

The Constitution of the White Earth Nation, and other native nations, were denatured by the plenary abrogation of the entente and treaties. The territorial domain of native sovereignty had been erased, and the precise constitutional prohibition of banishment was not enforceable.

Seven natives resisted the demise of governance, but we were immediately renounced and rebuked as extremists and exiled. The constitution was our only native trace of sovereignty, at the time, so we resorted to a diplomatic strategy of continental native liberty provided by the great and everlasting peace treaty with New France.

Forty native nations were signatories to La Grande Paix de Montréal in 1701, and for about sixty years the treaty provided peace for natives, fur traders, and the citizens of New France. The exiles were eager to double back with stories of earlier treaties and continental liberty because our native constitutional governance had been denied by the plenary power of the United States Congress.

The Great Peace of Montréal recognized by name and formal negotiations, empire cues, signatures, and totemic marks the unmistakable sovereignty of native nations in New France, New England, and the Great Lakes.

Hole in the Storm seemed to envision scenes of native exile, but the situation of our banishment was not the same as Dogroy Beaulieu or the renunciation of the spectacular triptych. The *Casino Whalers on a Sea of Sovereignty* portrayed the mighty motion of waves, the sleaze of casino overseers, grotesque gamers over slot machines, and the catastrophe of native sovereignty.

The abrogation of the reservation treaty, rescission of the constitution and native governance, and our exile that autumn resulted in an escape cruise on the *Baron of Patronia*, that marvelous houseboat of survivance and native sovereignty. We became the new native expatriates of continental liberty on Lake of the Woods.

Justice Molly Crèche, Moby Dick, Savage Love, and the other exiles told memorable treaty tales, the tease and ironies of princely names, workaday mockery, and the giveaway contingencies of government. Federal treaties were always hazy but the stories of the exiles were buoyant, a mirage of birthrights, bogus advances of civilization, and the steady comic teases and parodies of federal agents for more than a century. The new treaty tales were easily derived from the new regime and obscure duties of the endorsement sectors.

Waasese was an innovative storier with lasers, those beams, shimmers, and emission of radiation but not words or paint. She created incredible holoscenes, the precise projection of light, the haunted scenes and figures over the reservations, lakes, and cities. Most of the laser images were familiar, George Washington, Geronimo, Mae West, John Wayne, Sitting Bull, Bob Dylan, and Neighbor Smithy who wore a Vine Deloria Peace Medal, for instance, were seen several times in natural motion with Diane Glancy, Sherman Alexie, Louise Erdrich, Joy Harjo, George Morrison, David Bradley, and many other native writers and painters over the White Foxy Casino.

Waasese earned her nickname, a flash of lightning, in a laser laboratory as a graduate student, and created a laser scene of presidents and prominent natives that reached over the Mississippi River near the University of Minnesota. The holoscenes were in motion, faded, and then vanished in the night sky.

Waasese was constantly teased, of course, and given several nicknames, Tree House, Laser Carpenter, Crazy Beam, Chicago, Timber Maven, and at last the native word Waasese. The Chicago nickname was a historical reference to the reservation white pine that had been cut to build the city. Some natives converted that nickname to *zhingwaak*, white pine, but Waasese, a wild flash of lightning, outlasted the other nicknames.

Chewy Browne, a native soprano in her nineties, a truly catchy treaty storier, was honored as a senior exile on the very night of our departure from a boat dock near the ruins of the Seven Clans Casino in Warroad, Minnesota. Chewy chanted the names of her nine fancy chickens that night, and then told stories about how the chickens had scurried and crapped on the roulette tables and outsmarted the security agents with elusive clucks, magical cackles, and crow boasts in the casino.

Native creation stories were visionary, never the same as treaty tales. The contrasts of creation, and the totemic union of animals were never counted down to the territorial metes and bounds of separatist reservations and the ruse of sovereignty. Fancy chickens, however, were both creation and treaty stories, and memorable scenes at the casino.

Chewy was a shaman with fancy chickens.

Justice Molly Crèche, a prudent storier of creatures and treaties, counted ancient natives by diseases, grieved over the agony of pared animals in the wild fur trade, and created a poignant metes and bounds of lethal outpost pathogens, that decimation of natives, and, at the same time, the ghastly estates of peltry.

"Natives once envisioned totemic associations, bears, wolves, sandhill cranes, but our ancestors were never the honorable escorts of animals in the fur trade. We are the storiers of conscience, cast aside, and yet natives must continue to nurture totemic associations, the auras, spirits, and shadows of animals," declared Justice Molly Crèche.

Homer Drayn, vice chancellor of the William Warren Community College, announced in a formal statement, "Justice Crèche might have become a high court justice, but the hearsay of wild sex with animals and conversion of the tribal court to beaver rights and bear necrostories regrettably ended an eminent judicial career."

Drayn was an edgy native lawyer and constant rival to serve on the constitutional court. He had actually initiated the vicious rumors that Justice Crèche was having sex with mongrels and wild animals.

"Justice Molly Crèche always honored the standing of beaver, bear, moles, gypsy moths, juncos, spiders, and little brown bats in court," chanted Moby Dick.

"Crèche was right, she was always right about the rights of animals and their day in court," said Gichi Noodin, the steady voice of Panic Radio. "The trouble was, most natives worried more about the casino than about totems, mongrels, or fur trade animals, and the honorable justice was burdened with more cases and testimony about casino sleeve dogs than abandoned and abused children."

The White Earth Reservation was created by treaty on March 19, 1867. Minnesota had been a state for almost nine years when the federal government carved out a section of woodland and lakes for a reservation. That thorny episode of state separatism has never been a pleasurable source of native memories or stories, and for more than a century the treaty has never been a reliable warranty, never a true celebration of democracy, only a mockery of sovereignty and continental liberty.

Most natives remember the treaty tales and frightful situations when entire families were separated from their customary haunts, homes, and ventures, and relocated elsewhere on a federal reservation. The native resistance to separatism and treaty relocation was hardly recorded in national archives or state histories. The chronicles most celebrated were about the romance of the ancient fur trade, and favored timber barons who carried away the red and white pine on the White Earth Reservation.

Yet, in the face of constant government betrayals and crafty policies, natives endured and created an extraordinary democratic constitution, one of the prominent constitutions of the modern world, and resolved the devious mandates and feudal cache of saintly blood that was touted as the authentic trace and determination of native identities. Now, after two decades of autonomous governance our native state and constitution has been terminated, and the very protectors of the revered charter were exiled with a cast aside constitution.

The Constitution of the White Earth Nation, approved by a referendum of native citizens about twenty years ago, proclaims in the preamble that the Anishinaabe were the successors of a great tradition of continental liberty, a native constitution of families and totemic associations. These very principles and sentiments of native sovereignty and liberty would continue in a state of exile.

Justice Molly Crèche initiated at the same time as the egalitarian native government the White Earth Continental Congress, a native association that soon grew to more than three thousand members around the world. The Congress celebrated the creative achievements of natives since the establishment of the White Earth Reservation.

The Dominion of Canada was established four months later on July 1, 1867, and that day of independence has been celebrated every year. The coincidence of these three crucial events in continental culture and history, the Great Peace of Montréal, the congressional separation of natives and later abrogation of the reservation treaty, and the observance of dominion liberty, provided a chance to resolve the injustice of our exile, and secure the vision of the Constitution of the White Earth Nation.

The Canadian envoys of foreign and aboriginal affairs, national defense, and immigration were scheduled to arrive by boat to consider our formal petition to reconsider the original surveys and confusion over the international border, liberate the Northwest Angle as the Angle of Native Liberty, and secure Fort Saint Charles on Manidooke Minis, an island of spiritual power, as a native state, and to provide support and sanctuary for eight political exiles and the Constitution of the White Earth Nation.

The preliminary negotiations were scheduled on the deck of the *Baron of Patronia*, and later on Manidooke Minis. The Canadian envoys and agencies indicated they would consider the situation of eight exiles and native continental liberty. Summaries of the discussions would be broadcast nightly on Panic Radio.

The Canadian government acknowledged our fur trade ancestors and petition of ancient treaty rights to Fort Saint Charles, the first western post in the colonial province of New France. Pierre Gaultier de La Vérendrye, the military officer and trader, established and named the post in 1732 in honor of Charles de Beauharnois, Governor of New France. Canada mistakenly allowed the survey of the international boundary to include Northwest Angle, Fort Saint Charles, and other native land and islands in Minnesota.

The native exiles were remembered only by earned nicknames. Archive, the first narrator, poet, and novelist, Gichi Noodin, Great Wind, Captain of the *Baron of Patronia* and spirited broadcast voice of Panic Radio, Savage Love, an irony dog trainer and innovative unpublished writer, Moby Dick, exotic publisher and totemic guardian of deformed aquarium fish, Waasese, a laser holoscene scientist, Hole in the Storm, a visionary artist who earned an ironic nickname because he was a quiet painter at the very heart of a storm, Chewy Browne, the senior exile with a magnificent soprano voice, and Justice Molly Crèche, fur trade necrostorier and the steadfast advocate of totemic justice and animal rights in courts, declared a new native nation in exile at Fort Saint Charles in Lake of the Woods.

Chewy Beaulieu Browne was a delegate, twenty years ago, to the constitutional conventions, and she initiated the community councils and totemic associations that were essential to democratic governance. "If you ain't tookin then I'm a lookin," she loudly teased my great-uncle at the first convention, and he was taken, but they became very close friends and active in the community and totemic councils. Chewy enchanted the delegates then and the exiles now with her course of teases and emotive soprano voice. She sang the poetry of the preamble and the articles about irony and continental liberty.

Chewy was one of the thirteen Manidoo Singers. The singers honored the spirits of the dead with songs, including the despised governor of the sector, Godtwit Moon. She was determined at age ninety to live in exile, and would not be denied the right of exile on the *Baron of Patronia*.

Moby Dick started the ouster stories on the first voyage of exiles that autumn. The notice of our actual banishment was a handprinted poster mounted at the entrance to the casino. The poster noted that we were removed forever from the former reservation and new federal sector. The order was arbitrary, and everyone understood that we were ostracized only because we had resisted the congressional abrogation of the constitution and egalitarian governance, declared our confidence and absolute allegiance to the native constitution, and because of our wholehearted loyalty to new totemic associations, but not the national sectors.

Many natives returned to live on the reservation the same year the constitution was certified by almost eighty percent of the registered citizens who voted in a referendum. There was great excitement at the time, election debates were serious and constructive, several native judges of the constitutional court were confirmed, totemic associations and councils were underway, and the new library collection had more than doubled with the novels, poetry, history, art, and critical studies published by native authors.

The eager delegates to the constitutional conventions initiated the new custom of Treaty Shirts on the same day that native citizens endorsed the Constitution of the White Earth Nation. The eight exiles carried on that shirty tribute to native governance for twenty years and wore the same unwashed shirt at conferences and legislative sessions, a ceremonial vestment of continental liberty. The odors of the shirts were nasty, and the conventions and native seminar stains were ironic archives, the traces and citations of hors d'oeuvres, silhouettes of chicken wings, spicy meatballs at banquets, and buffet spatters.

Tedwin Makwa, or The Bear, a native philosopher, was our garment mentor, and he was renowned for the stench of his embroidered cowboy shirt. He wore the same unwashed shirt at conferences, social and political events, and in the classroom for decades. Traces of his travels and activities, overnight binges, messy sex, pizza and burger prints, stains of mustard, wine, mayonnaise, and fry bread ooze were the distinctive codes of cryptic stories and native reciprocity.

Makwa was truly a master of ironic stories, but only strangers, the uninitiated, or those with olfactory disorder would sit next to him at a conference or a restaurant. The stench of his cowboy shirt with more than a decade of sweat, grease, and wine would foul the air and overpower any ordinary conversation. Friends held their breath when he reached out for a hearty embrace.

The Constitution of the White Earth Nation was set more than sixty years too late in any critical calendar of continental liberty. Earlier the constitutional government could have become much stronger with the actual steady growth and prosperity of the nation rather than with the slow decline of the world economy and financial systems. The economic decline resulted in the abrogation of the reservation treaty and the ruination of the Constitution of the White Earth Nation.

There were many earlier native initiatives to create a democratic constitution, the very visions and strategies that would have connected with the first wave of native college graduates in the nineteen sixties, but the steady political putter and shame of federal agents, and the obvious trickery, lethargy, and corruption of older reservation leaders were too much to counter at the time.

Twenty years ago hundreds of natives returned with their relatives to the reservation, to a new constitutional democracy, with praise and anticipation of an ethical and worthy government. We were right about the merit, ethos, and virtues of autonomous governance, but never gave much thought to the reports on the incredible race of credit and the national debt. We had overlooked the enormous increase in trust endorsements, once-named entitlements, and regulations, and the worldwide government debt and economic decline. The conditions became so serious in the past decade that some news and editorial reports declared the crises an era of political retractions, banishment and renouncement, a "national dust bowl of endorsements," public obligations and debts, debts, debts.

Children, elders, horses, pets, boats, summer cabins, snowmobiles, stores, movie theaters, markets, malls, and houses were abandoned in the millions around the country, and we were banished along with an autonomous native government when treaty land and reservations were converted overnight to federal endorsement sectors by congressional plenary power.

Clément Beaulieu, my great-uncle, pointed out this giant double catch of plenary power when the constitution was ratified, a tricky catch we did not fully grasp at the time, that congressional actions could terminate the reservation and leave the constitution without a native venue, domain, or territory to practice governance.

Plenary power was absolute, but not comparable to the elusive traces and turns of demons in native trickster stories. The conversion of reservations and state counties to federal sectors was actually ironic because we had been weakened by our own vitality, gentle conceit, and hearty determination to create a constitutional government. We were convinced at the time that the honor of a democratic constitution would never be denied in the modern world.

Savage Love avowed that the word "abandonment is an absence, a passive accusation, inactive, and the words oust, banish, evict, exile, and chase were active, but neither the post nor promises were more than a tentative intention, and with no actual sense or significance, none." She was always casual, and seemed to understate the philosophy of existential absence over presence, and yet repeated the point that the ratified articles in the constitution were mere intentions, autonomous in practice, and we were the natives who created the actual substance with each word, and the most recent recitation was in the sentiments of exile.

"The constitution is more active in exile than it was bound to the territory of a federal treaty," Gichi Noodin shouted, "so, our exile made perfect sense, a constitution of new continental liberty."

"No, no, abandoned children and mongrels are actual, real, a heartbeat, a presence, not the same as moored boats and empty houses," moaned Moby Dick.

"The words have no meaning or native story," declared Savage Love. "The notions of abandon and renounce were never states of gravity because words were always stranded in emotion and nostalgia, and the tease of the next listener or reader, the word was never an actual person, mongrel, or totem, the words are naught but a crease of sound."

"Right, the meaning of the words in the constitution change with the users, and in the same way that stories on Panic Radio were never, never the same," said Gichi Noodin. "Why would natives listen day after day if the stories were always the same?"

"Children and animals, abandoned or not, have real names and legal standing in the world court of justice, but repossessed cars and foreclosed houses do not," said Justice Molly Crèche.

"Cars and abandoned machines were never sincere," said Hole in the Storm, "but the great spirit of animals have standing in art and any serious native court of stories."

"The bat and animal totems double the standing of humans," said Waasese. "The totems were envisioned and animals and bats have always been the reserved traces in our stories and the precedent of courts."

"Names, machines, death, empty, no meaning, nothing, death nothing, names nothing, words are not an absence and not a salvation or memory, words are created and last only in the moment of a tease or shout," said Savage Love.

Maybe, but the stories of the exiles in *Treaty Shirts* were eternal, and in the same way the articles in our constitution have always had meaning. The words were in the clouds that love to hear a native dream song. We were banished, seven constitutioneers with exile nicknames, outside of the federal sectors, and yet the ironic stories of our names, and posted notices of our exile, have meaning and significance.

"Nothing more than native nostalgia, no significance," declared Savage Love. She smiled, and raised one hand in silence, a gesture of patience and respect as one of the seven exiles, and then turned and walked away with five great exiled irony mongrels, Wild Rice, Sardine, Mother Teresa, Mutiny, and White Favor.

Savage Love earned her nickname as a tribute to the crusty mother of the poet and novelist Samuel Beckett of Dublin and Paris. Savage Love was an innovative novelist, and actually better suited to exile than a commune. She was the direct descendant of Chance, the sensitive and honorable native healer who taught dozens of mongrels how to detect the absence of irony. That has been an eminent practice, and more significant than any prayers for deliverance or the promissory politics of the federal government.

Chance and Savage Love were born on treaty land, but were never connected to a community. They lived with the artist Dogroy Beaulieu and several mongrel healers on the Pale of the White Earth Reservation and were ridiculed in stories. Chance, Savage Love, and the mongrels moved with Dogroy to the Gallery of Irony Dogs in Minneapolis.

Chewy and the seven exiles were banished along with sex criminals, dogs, and domestic pets. The federal sector banned the mere possession of dog food, and imposed work fines for those who were caught feeding birds, cats, or dogs. Mongrels, the great healers of natives, were abandoned in the hundreds on the sector, and were driven to search the overnight casino trash for food with the rowdy crows. The mature mongrels truly protected the weaker and dependent designer breeds on the sector. Three abandoned and dirty white Bichon Frisé, and several other catchy named terriers, learned how to carry on with the pure mongrels, and with the tricky manners of sector survivors.

The abandoned mongrels ran in packs and rehearsed their lonely nightly howls near the treelines. The timber wolves disregarded the mongrel howls. The wild distance of so many domestic generations could not be overcome even with a practiced bay. The renounced miniature sleeve dogs were thwarted with the genes of insider pedigrees, but they ran happily with the pure mongrels, forever burdened with a shallow, anxious, and inane yelp, yelp, yelp.

"Mongrels never abandon their young, or any young dogs, pedigree or not, deformed or not," said Moby Dick.

Mongrels have never forgotten their origins and easily grasped the meaning of irony and abandonment on the sector. The mongrels were healers, and have endured the curses, sorrow, and endearment of humans for thousands of years.

Savage Love worried that the five mongrels at her side would only appreciate the words *abandonment* and *rescue* in ironic stories, and bark at the absence of irony. Mongrels at casino dumpsters, and the creepy poses and declarations of sector toadies and politicians, were obtuse and truly ironic and the absence deserved a bark, but mongrel barks were banned and dangerous.

Savage Love declared that "only a cruel and benighted separatist would abandon our healers and great pointers of the absence of irony, or name a mongrel Cracker, Custer, Cur, Crud, Abandon, or Renounce, without a native tease and astute sense of irony."

The mission priests created mundane and descriptive nicknames of mongrels in the early years of the reservation, White Paws, Big Spot, Bud, Joe, Kim, Gordy, Catch, Pickle, Manypenny, and Bear Heart. The mission sisters shunned the mongrels and wild animals, but demonstrated their love of native children and tolerated the redeemed mongrels, the shy mongrels that never nosed a holy crotch. Luckily the ecclesiastic nicknames of mongrels on the reservation were never Vice, Shame, Salvation, or Black Devil.

I was a novelist in the generous literary shadow of my great-uncle who wrote the constitution, and more than thirty books about natives. Most of the natives who returned to the reservation that first year of the constitution were trained and experienced teachers, lawyers, athletes, medical doctors, corporate accountants, an electronic engineer, a pirate radio broadcaster, an artist, fireman, musician, and a holographic artist and scientist. Rightly, we were always teased as constitutional newcomers and earned our nicknames based on manner, habits, diversions, and we sometimes earned more than one. The newcomers were commonly known on the reservation by their nicknames.

Surely our loyalties and constitutional allegiance were not cultural crimes that deserved banishment or termination. The principles of governance were abused and discredited by sleazy sector autocrats, and yet we could not deny that arbitrary decisions and policies were common for more than a century and sometimes celebrated in the modern ruins of continental liberty.

The visionary stories, treaty deceptions, and cultural ruins were never the same from one generation to the next, and the cultural conversion of casinos was only a proem to the extreme political narratives of national endorsements and the strange revisions of penalties and justice.

La Maison de Torture Extraordinaire, for instance, a reversal in the national practice of torture, would surely be more bearable than archaic political evictions, religious torture, and secret rendition strategies. The outcome would be the same but the new torture of solicitude caused no nightmares, psychic scars, or political crises. Separation with compassion, or banishment with no body trauma, was nothing less than removal and exile. There was no virtue in the cruel irony that our native ancestors endured arbitrary and malicious separation carried out by federal agents in the early years of the White Earth Reservation.

The exiles were descendants of the fur trade, and our ancestors once declared their loyalty to the French in the empire wars. Today, with loathsome stories and dreadful memories of the fur trade, we bear the surnames, totemic nicknames, and cultural distinctions of native exiles, and to create a new union with the spirits of animals we initiated totemic associations and constitutional councils to advise the new government. The original totems were created in the spirit of the animals, in ancestral stories of natural reason, the turns of seasons, eternal migrations of birds, and the common array and motion of wolf spiders, cicadas, bobcats, bats, kingfishers, carpenter ants, cedar waxwings, moccasin flowers, praying mantis, and coywolves.

Clément Beaulieu was a delegate and the principal writer of the Constitution of the White Earth Nation. Article Five provided that "freedom of thought and conscience, academic and artistic irony, and literary expression shall not be denied, violated or controverted by the government."

The Anishinaabe told great trickster stories of creation and enticement, teases and quirky mercy, and scenes of visionary motion. These memorable stories were never translated rightly in the book, but natives have the moral imagination, the lure of totemic associations, the natural justice of stories and literary irony forever in the Constitution of the White Earth Nation, and in the ancient legacy of the Great Peace of Montréal.

Only a native constitution would include a clear and direct reference to artistic irony. My great-uncle wrote that the constitution must encourage ironic stories and art, create new totems, more than the mere imitation of the traditional birds and animals, and he specified that the totemic and community councils should "strengthen the philosophy of *mino-bimaadiziwin*, to live a good life, and in good health, through the creation and formation of associations, events and activities that demonstrate, teach and encourage respect, love, bravery, humility, wisdom, honesty and truth for citizens." That good life, however, would never absolve the cruelty and spiritual abuse of animals in the fur trade. The cultural memory of dead totemic animals was unforgiven, never a constitutional clemency.

The new totems and cultural burdens of natives were hardly significant when compared with the decimation of animals, and demise of the original totemic associations in the furious continental fur trade of the past three centuries. No national separation strategy, treaty deceit, constitution, dominion, tiresome overcompensations of monotheism, or the romantic tread of enlightenment could absolve the outright cruelty and slaughter of animals for felt hats and furry fashions in Europe.

Our new totems and the constitutional associations that were founded in the name of wolf spiders, coywolves, bats, bobcats, deformed fish, and moccasin flowers, would never reconcile the native cruelty to the great spirits of the animals, and the mass murder of beaver, bear, marten, ermine, and deer in centuries of the fur trade. Some city squirrels, raccoons, caged birds, and most mongrels continue to trust humans, even after dogs were banished from the federal sector, but the spirits of the beaver and other animals remain forever distant and deny humans the right to hear their remarkable stories of survivance. Truly the spirits of the animals await the tragic outcome of human civilization.

Justice Molly Crèche protected the rights of animals in the courtroom, and she was the only jurist who honored the memory of the animals murdered in the fur trade. She argued that because so many animals were brought close to extinction, "necrostories, the testimony of native totemic associations, and hearsay of animal genocide were accepted as evidence in the courtroom." Crèche continued to hear testimony in exile, and the court stories of exile were broadcast on Panic Radio.

Our totemic associations and heartfelt observance of natural motion were clearly a philosophy of *bimaadiziwin*, but the beaver would never again enable humans to stand in their daily presence and survivance culture or participate in their trust and natural duty.

The pushy game hunters resented the new totems of spiders, birds, bats, insects, and wild flowers, and at the same time they protected timber wolves. The poseurs were furious that the word *wolf* was specifically used in the constitutional totemic association of the coywolves and wolf spiders. The outward manly totems correlated directly with metal clamp traps, heavy weapons, bright lights, snow machines, and giant pickup trucks.

Mostly the catcalls, curses, and politics of resentment were concentrated on the actual constitution, the very ethical provisions of governance that denied the easy dominance of the tradition fascists and Midewin Messengers. The fascists favored a circular patriarchy, a fishy patchwork tradition of absolute authority, and conspired against the constitutional elections. They continued to undermine every practice of egalitarian governance. The fascists harkened to invented traditions, and perverted the sacred *midewiwin*, an obscure medicine dance, and an association of healers and great visionaries. So, the heavy hunters and traditioneers were eager to join the faction of authoritarian managers in the new federal sector. The blood count connivers emerged to reign over native identities a second time in reservation history.

No, we were not romantic utopians, crazed, or wanton state criminals. The national reports that we had committed a murder, violated the federal charter of sector migration, or simply traveled without permission, and disabled the drone monitors were not true. Our inherent and constitutional liberties were denied, and we were brazenly threatened by the new governor to vacate the old reservation and the new federal endorsement sector.

The Constitution of the White Earth Nation clearly prohibited banishment, yet we were ousted and our rights violated by a corrupt autocrat and private security agents twenty years after the constitution was set in motion with native citizens.

Precisely, we were removed, as our ancestors had once been ordered by federal agents to leave the treaty boundary of the reservation more than a century earlier for publishing the *Progress*, the first independent native newspaper critical of federal policies.

Paradoxically we were banished at the very same time that native children were taught the ethics and principles of the democratic constitution in nearby public schools, and many citizens carried a miniature copy of the egalitarian document as a native prompt of liberty. The dubious ethics of federal policies had actually advanced to a new level of hypocrisy. Native sovereignty and the doctrine of reserved rights were never mentioned or considered in the political conversion of treaty reservations and counties into federal trust endorsements sectors.

Waasese created marvelous laser holoscenes, lively and magical light shows, and the radiant scenes easily diverted the drones and distracted the sector security agents. The Specter Drones, aerial monitors, and miniature digital cameras were everywhere, mounted in trees and beams, at the casino, underwater, and in books, tablets and toilets, and managed by private surveillance agencies to detect and track human motion in the sector, but the silent drones could not always detect an actual native from a laser scene.

Yes, we rightly teased, tormented, and menaced but never murdered the first governor of the White Earth Sector of the National Sectors and Trust Endorsements. Godtwit Moon had already earned three descriptive nicknames, Mosey, for his casual manner when he was paroled to the casino, Husky for the color of his eyes that changed from luminous blue to amber, and Miskojaane for his bulbous red nose. He was a poseur, boozer, and vicious conniver who concocted native traditions in a federal prison, and was secretly paroled to the reservation through a new and ironic rendition strategy of generous treatment.

Godtwit Moon was released from federal prison in the last three months of his criminal sentence for larceny, extortion, possession of narcotics, and weapons violations, and moved to the new Saint Cloud La Maison de Torture Extraordinaire. The new regime of empathy and solicitude was a complete reversal of earlier torture and security rendition programs.

The French academies had prescribed more humane remedies, care and compassion, and *Rendition de Gentillesse* to counter the previous abuses and extreme renditions of narcotic, electric, digital, radiance, audio trauma, and the notorious torture of waterboarding.

Godtwit Moon and other poseurs extraordinaire learned how to practice a perverted and concise version of the native *midewiwin*, a sacred, obscure, and traditional dance. The new rendition prisoners were otherwise placated, exploited and completely overcome with daily doses of sincerity, shrewdly soothed and stupefied with praise, sympathy, tolerance, and manly candor, the four cardinal principles of the new state strategy of moderate corrections and *Rendition de Gentillesse*.

Gentle, meditative music was transmitted throughout the day and night in the rendition prison. Enya was the most common music of the night, the merciful music of solemnity. "Thank Heaven for Little Girls," by Maurice Chevalier, "You're Nobody till Somebody Loves You," by Dean Martin, crooner of the casino Rat Pack, the resonance of violins by Mantovani, and Yanni compositions were selected for new affect encounter sessions on ordinary care, the tender touch and gaze, tease of truth and trust, notable pleasure words, cautious generosity, and other soothing music and meditative cues and voices were broadcast in distinct sessions on leadership styles and legal sexuality.

The alterable prisoners who completed the program were frequently hired by social services agencies to soothe the many worries of the elderly in sector hospitals and nursing homes, an ironic and creepy continuance of the extraordinary rendition instituted in France.

Godtwit Moon completed the rendition program, an anxious but clever softhearted poseur, and he was released early to the custody of the corporate manager of the White Foxy Casino on the White Earth Nation.

Godtwit chased the casino money, an easy maneuver, and was promoted for his gentle poses of native culture and compassion as a supervisor of the bars, restaurants, and slot machines. Strategically he devised a way to decrease the payout to gamblers, aerate the daily entrée at the three restaurants, water the drinks, and was promoted regularly by the casino management company. Some four years later he was nominated, for no other reason than his native poses and simulated casino compassion, to serve as the first governor of the new federal endorsement sector.

The native outrage over the conversion of the treaty reservation to an entitlement sector was only equal to the contempt for the arbitrary promotion of the new rendition parolee Godtwit Moon. The poseur never hesitated to simulate his praise of the heartfelt constitution and at the same time revel in the very ruins of an established and representative native government.

Godtwit arbitrarily retired seven dedicated casino employees, and the very next day he hired five parolees from Saint Cloud La Maison de Torture Extraordinaire as personal security sentries. The second night of his new reign he changed the official name of the White Foxy Casino to the Coy Care Casino, a new services institution of the National Sectors and Trust Endorsements.

Casino sovereignty was recognized more than sixty years ago, and most reservation casinos near urban areas became wealthy. The money, hundreds of millions of dollars, was actually a crafty switch or transfer of wealth from the losers to natives and casino managers, an ironic hand over of a mea culpa culture, considered regret money at the time. That huge transfer of wealth from ordinary citizens, mostly the elderly, and chronic gamers, was terminated overnight with the congressional abrogation of the treaties. The White Foxy Casino was a minor contender in the huge transfer of wealth to native casinos.

The Indian Gaming Regulatory Act meant to protect and monitor native casinos, but the basic notion was curious, even mistaken, that gambling was a traditional practice of native cultures. Rightly, games of chance were common, and enhanced with music, cultural teases, and ceremonies, but that communal pleasure does not directly relate to slot machines, and the avarice of casinos.

The White Foxy Casino was terminated by plenary power along with the treaty reservation and constitution, and the contingent legislation provided a rescue conversion of casinos to corporate contract ventures that would serve native and other citizens in sectors of endorsements. The original management company of the casino continued as the federal contract agency to carry out the new sector endorsement programs.

Straightaway natives nicknamed the security sentries the Peace Hookers. Godtwit and the Peace Hookers became the subject of the most exotic trickster stories, a natural respite from the ironies of rendition and sector politics. The elders were eager to share wider and more mature stories about the early nicknames of nasty federal agents. The *niinag mangindibe*, or dick head, the big head penis stories, were the most popular that first autumn of sector dominance. The Peace Hookers were monster dick heads in the new trickster stories.

Godtwit Moon was obviously despised, and feared, mocked, shunned, and sidestepped, but seldom teased because the native tease was truly a communal gesture of tentative and uncertain compassion. The tradition fascists and native toadies praised the heavy management style of the sector governor, the whims of gentle rage, and every sensible native citizen was evasive and renounced the very presence of the new sector poseurs.

The National Sectors and Trust Endorsements at White Earth converted the White Foxy Casino Hotel to the Coy Care Resident Hotel for native elders and disabled citizens, and the convention conference rooms became a medical services center. Many elder residents were relocated from nearby cities to the Coy Care Casino.

The social security and federal disability payments to some elders, the gamers and residents, were deposited directly to an account in the Coy Care Casino Bank. Godtwit was president, of course, of the new sector bank. Many native elders were very pleased to live in the hotel residence, eat at the three casino restaurants, and easily walk or motor in a chair to the slot machines. The standard gaming rules were revised to eliminate actual money and citizens were issued electronic tags with casino credit.

The native players received monthly credit points that could be won or lost at the slot machines, poker, blackjack, and other games. Clearly almost every player was expected to lose, but the automatic credits regulated the debt of elder players, and those who lost their monthly credits were obligated to work at the casino or resident hotel, and others on road crews or at sector institutions to restore the credits. Every sector native was required to work for endorsements and to restore with hourly labor the total monthly debts on Coy Casino Credit Tags.

Most natives who feared Godtwit and the Peace Hookers were cautious and only conspired to partake in cynical gossip, as cautious as they were about the taunt and curse of shamans, and reckoned at times with the whisperers and scandalmongers. That combination of nasty gossip and shamanic torments had chased away many federal agents and pompous poseurs in the past, but the new sector governor and management, shadows of the national debt, and severe economic decline would never be absolved with testy rumors. The sector haters and native exiles, however, were resolute about the removal of the rendition governor.

The Shaman Crease, a notorious and covert circle of native healers and tent shakers created and vigilantly distributed the magical Waaban Blue Union, untraceable narcotic concoctions, and at the same time practiced natural and traditional herbal remedies. The healers invited the exiles, several other dancers, and the showy sector governor to an ecstatic overnight dance and spectacular light show at the Boy Scout Camp at Many Point Lake.

The seven exiles wore Treaty Shirts that mysterious and unpredictable night, the same stained shirts that we wore at the ratification of the constitution, the sector revision of the reservation, and notice of our banishment. Treaty Shirts embodied our spirit, sweat, and loyalty to the constitution, and we wore the shirts unwashed at every convention and convocation in the past twenty years.

Godtwit Moon was distracted by our presence at the dance, of course, and tried to disguise his worries that we were there to curse him in our Treaty Shirts, but suddenly he smiled, turned his head to the side, and waved his hands to show compassion, surely a cynical gesture of *Rendition de Gentillesse,* the new politics of compassion.

Savage Love tied blue treaty bandanas around the necks of the mongrels of irony, and yet we worried that the governor might execute another ban of mongrels at the dance. The five mongrels smiled at the sector governor, a much wiser ironic and totemic version of rendition. The mongrels were designated healers in blue bandanas.

White Favor was a whistler, not a moaner, a whistler with a clear pitch, and that night he whistled several times at Godtwit and the two Peace Hookers who were invited to the dance at Many Point Lake.

The Debwe Heart Dance, an ecstatic native cavort of truth, was slightly revised that night to deceive the hefty autocrat who could hardly walk through the casino twice without turning slightly blue with worry and heart fatigue. The drumbeats and heart bounces were slowed, and a new cast of songs and stories were simulated and shortened in his honor, only the most common names of nature, white pine, cedar, sumac, waxwing, beaver, porcupine, and water moccasins. The governor was cornered in a circle of tricky shamans who chanted these common names with a clever curse and poetic simplicity.

Savage Love taunted the governor with stories about the extraordinary rendition of words, the gentle words of death, and the ecstasy of nothing, absolutely nothing, not a single thing, and she encouraged him to inhale a hefty mound of blue luminous powder served on a short cedar stave. Godtwit sniffed and reached for Savage Love, but she ducked and moved between the trees.

The Specter Drones circled the red pine and were seduced by the holoscenes of historical figures over the lake. Waasese projected three images of Distinguished Eagle Scouts, Gerald Ford, president, Neil Armstrong, astronaut, and Steven Spielberg, movie director, in honor of the Many Point Boy Scout Camp, and Christopher Columbus, Samuel de Champlain, Cotton Mather, Andrew Jackson, Chief Joseph, Geronimo, Babe Ruth, Hillary Clinton, Vladimir Putin, and the waxy laser crucifixion of Jesus Christ slowly vanished in a wave on the lake.

The Peace Hookers and other sector security agents were amused but not distracted by the laser shows. The agents, however, were scared away from the truth dance by nasty packs of feral mongrels.

Godtwit Moon inhaled the narcotic and promptly lost his practiced rendition poses. He became belligerent, smoky faced, and shouted two mundane heart dance versions of truth, "slot machines and fast sex," and "hate cats, hate dirty pets," and then he danced in the red pines near the shoreline of Many Point Lake. The poseur circled in the dark, sniffed the last trace of blue shine on his finger, and hallucinated the presence of native women, naked natives in magical flight. Wild Rice howled at the poseur and nosed his swollen gray ankles. His heart was weakened by subdued rage, and his crotch was stained with urine.

White Favor whistled a lively tune, and with other moans and bays the mongrels created a magical chorus in the red pine that night. Mutiny turned and brushed her lacy ginger tail on the thick thighs of the governor.

Packs of feral mongrels circled the heart dancers and growled at the treeline, an escape distance. The bright eyes of the mongrels flashed in the red pine, ten, twenty or more mongrels in natural motion. Sardine gestured with her wet nose, and we were convinced the pack was rightly tracking their prey, the paunchy governor of the sector.

Waasese created later that night holoscenes of erotic monks with various animals above the birch and red pine near the lake, scenes from stories in the *Manabosho Curiosa*, an ancient and obscure manuscript published by Moby Dick. The wide circulation of the erotic monk stories, and the indisputable allegiance to the constitution were the obvious cause of his banishment. The tradition fascists were clearly aroused and outraged, of course, at the sex scenes with timber wolves and bears, and because the publisher was a constitutional loyalist, had collected and nurtured deformed aquarium fish, and earned the nickname of a great white whale. White, the ordinary name of a pigment surely made the poseurs more anxious than the giant whale of fiction by Herman Melville.

Moby Dick had nurtured deformed fish in two huge aquariums at the White Foxy Casino, conspicuously located near the center of the slot machines. The deformed fish were given names of famous explorers. Christopher Columbus shimmered with four fancy pelvic fins, and Matteo Ricci swerved to the side with huge floppy pectoral fins. Jeanne Baret, the explorer and naturalist, was a bright, sociable goldfish with five dorsal fins. The new gamers paused at the machines and watched the magical motion of contorted fish in the enormous curved tanks. The fish were exceptional, double heads and dorsal fins, triple eyes, bent spines, marbled, spotted, and hideous overbites. The tank was backlighted and hues of blue shivered through the water. The curious fish nosed the thick glass, deformed even more by the magnification, and stared at the faces of the casino losers.

Moby Dick maintained the deformed fish were the modern art of nature, the fancy of abstract expressionism, a tease and creative crease of ancestry, although the artistic expression of four eyes, or three dorsal fins in natural motion were no more grotesque that the disabled gamers with oxygen tanks on the outside of the aquariums.

Waasese projected a blue laser bear and several monks masturbating, and other monks shimmered in a natural sense of motion and embraced cottontail rabbits. A monk with wild hair touched the moist underbelly of a gentle beaver. The holoscenes overhead, visions and mirages, and the devious dance of truth on the shoreline, were followed later with an incredible incident of vengeance and death.

Godtwit Moon turned his head from side to side, and traced with his finger the scenes of erotic motion that clear autumn night at Many Point Lake. Later the poseur was slowly squished to death under the light cleated tracks of a snow machine. No one would reveal who drove the machine back and forth several times over the bloody body of the sector governor. The face was crushed, and the heavy arms of the poseur twitched in one direction of the track, and the chest wheezed in the other direction.

The elusive pack of feral mongrels moved closer to the snow machine and one by one, patched mongrels and three pedigree miniatures, nosed the mashed remains of the sector governor. Some of the mongrels moaned, others sneezed, and rolled over in the moist weeds. The Bichon Frisé and a hairy Chihuahua whined over the body, and then ran away in silence.

Many natives had imagined nasty ways to murder the sector governor, but crushed by a snow machine was never mentioned as a strategy. One storier staked the poseur overnight for the wolves, but only vultures might consider his mushy, sour flesh. Moby Dick told one of the best stories, the slow submersion of the sector governor into the casino aquarium with deformed fish. Savage Love thought his body parts should be returned in small plastic sandwich bags to La Maison de Torture Extraordinaire. Gichi Noodin moved for an ironic banquet of cured sector governor on a sacrificial stake.

My fantasy of the murder was much more elaborate and lasted longer than the crush of snow machine tracks. Godtwit Moon was bound in clear plastic and strapped into a microlight aircraft with the controls set to run out of gas over the border lakes in Canada. That wicked governor might have flown for about two hours and vanished as a dead exile in Rainy Lake.

Neighbor Smithy, the curious nickname of the newly elected president, became the most recent political amateur to mismanage the burdens of the national economy. Smithy narrowly defeated the rich and pragmatic incumbent who had extensive corporate, legal, legislative, and foundation experience. The malaise and misery of citizens resulted in very low numbers of voters in elections. The political parties focused only on voters selected by computer algorithms, electronic names and party recognition, and with instant cash eased the burden of voters who could enter a password and touch any monitor or computer screen to vote for the president.

Smithy was elected by a bare majority of voters who touched his name on voice activated phones provided by the new endorsement programs. The new president assured the nation with ironic words of honor and truth at an electronic inauguration that he would restyle the crush of the economy into "a natural native transparency" to deliver and serve trust endorsements to the "good folks of the country." The cozy word "folks" was an obscure word to most voters, but the manner of the electronic message was rather tedious and folksy. The "natural native" in his endorsement maneuver was unintended irony. His presidency and the endorsement programs were sardonic, a great tradition of nothing, or at best the absence that meant only the politics of a promissory destiny.

The president was wordy and carried out executive orders with audacity, and with the support of congressional plenary power, the wild and capricious reconstruction of the entire economy. He boldly counteracted the enormous fiscal burdens of hundreds of heavily regulated and over-strained programs with a complete radical revision of the delivery of trust endorsements to eligible citizens in major cities, towns, counties, enclaves, and former treaty reservations around the country. The executive and plenary revisions were plainly political, bureaucratic protocols that would not directly reduce the national debt. The remedial objectives were nothing more than a clumsy strategy to reduce the direct burden of administration, contract services to selected companies, and to abrogate native treaties.

The federal treaty of March 19, 1867, that established the metes and bounds of the White Earth Reservation was abrogated after a hundred and sixty-seven years. Congress debated for only three days and then voted with plenary power to entirely revoke native treaties that early afternoon on October 22, 2034. The survey boundary of federal reservations and established counties in the states were converted at once to federal sectors of services and trust endorsements.

Congress hesitated with only slight resistance to the president and then enacted with a bare majority vote a comprehensive and structural revision of federal governance to manage the enormous national obligation and growing debt for medical services, disabilities, social security, public education, federal employment, military veterans, federal retirement, interstate roads and bridges, pendant phones, and other federal endorsements created in the past several decades. The security and defense of the country was not included in the debates on the national debt.

The congressional plenary power and constitutive legislation proclaimed in a single sentence the abrogation of reservation treaties. Truly, the entire national conversion of trust endorsements was presented in only nineteen words and the date of commencement, and with unbelievable concision and clarity. "National trust endorsements shall be administered, regulated, and delivered by governors of designated counties and terminated reservation sectors, commencing October 22, 2034."

The White Earth Reservation became one of the sectors to deliver the consolidated services of the National Sectors and Trust Endorsements. That incredible announcement was simultaneously released on every public and personal computer and on miniature news monitors by means of state and national surveillance services of Tracebeat and State Chips. The trust revision was more of a political siege than a new service, and most native citizens easily denounced the entire program.

Naturally, citizens everywhere were worried about their entitlements and new endorsements, and the many services promised by the federal government. These remote and abstract decisions, the congressional abrogation of treaties, and the crude termination of native sovereignty and constitutional governance were rather vague and unreal until the arrival a few days later of the contract surveillance agencies and the deployment of Specter Drones.

Sunday, October 22, 2034, obviously became a day of contrary memories, and the ironic stories of our banishment and insurgence would become a great literature of an exiled native nation. The native egalitarian descendants of the fur trade became the exiled citizens of a new nation in natural motion.

The Constitution of the White Earth Nation lost the sovereignty of jurisdiction when the original treaty was abrogated, and on that very same day my great-uncle, who was a delegate and wrote the actual constitution, celebrated his hundredth birthday with the seven exiles and many other admirers. On a cold night a few days later he walked alone into the solitude of the red pine forest and vanished near the headwaters of the Mississippi River.

Sunday, on the very same day the reservation treaty was abrogated, the White Foxy Casino sponsored the annual White Earth Animosh Pageant, a wild celebration of pure mongrels, and that afternoon the Radical Citizens of Peace and Ethnic Justice dedicated a giant bronze statue of Clyde Bellecourt, the controversial and dubious founder of the American Indian Movement, erected near the entrance to the Band Box Diner, a city landmark near Elliot Park in south Minneapolis. Bellecourt, who had served time in federal prison for violation of narcotics laws, was a distant episode of obtuse protests, the past tense of rough and ready bony ideologies, and a time of patsy liberal politics when the city mayor honored a paroled criminal for his service to the community. The most recent descendants and nostalgic associates of the radical leader, who had been mercifully forgotten in some twenty years, revised the stories of the activist and persuaded a foundation and state historical agency to resurrect in larger-than-life bronze the figure of Clyde Bellecourt.

Bellecourt, the bully man in a huge convertible, some seventy years earlier, had swiped the resistance of native communal activists in the city. The original activists had preceded him by decades, and yet the parolee convinced godly liberal and romantic congregations that native victimry was a radical strategy. Native humor, satire, and stories of reversals and poverty at the time became mere claims of entitlements and victimry.

The faults of aggrandizement were inexcusable, but enhanced identities were neither native nor heroic. The romantics, and radical revisionists, statue promoters, the churchy fundraisers, and the sculptor never seemed to understand that natives were communal at heart and not the heroic proxies of victimry.

The muscular bronze statue, a heroic simulation of victimry, was dedicated coincidentally on the same day that the federal government

30

announced the enactment of the vast sector endorsements and outright surveillance. Natives had been simulated for so long they became the very essence of exotic victimry. Even the critical narratives of assimilation policies and federal boarding schools contracted natives into fugitive scenes of tradition and tragedy.

The Animosh Pageant was reserved for pure mongrels, the only annual celebration that sidelined pedigree prancers and sleeve dogs. The mongrels danced on two paws, barked and bayed to various tunes and teases, smiled, toothy, silly grins, and rolled over, wiggled, and leaped and bounced with ballet moves, glissade, grand jeté, and pas de chat. No *gaazhagens*, or cat pageant, had ever been supported on the reservation, and later that week pets were banned by order of the new sector governor.

The most memorable performance at the last pageant was a murmur by four mongrels, a deep harmonic *om* or *aum*, a throat moan, not a purr or growl but an *om* hum that vibrated in the autumn air. The elders gathered to touch the hearts of the murmur mongrels and be healed. The other catchy performance was the calico mongrel that meowed, meowed, meowed as a cat. The mongrels moaned but never barked at the imitation of a cat. The mongrel pageant was broadcast live on various network streams, Principal Dogs, Canine Scenes, Mongrel Show Boats, Fetch Ballet, and Dog Meowsters. The mongrel *om* quartet was truly more famous that year than Neighbor Smithy.

The Animosh Pageant was a critical distraction that autumn because the new sector management and service conventions generated a great panic on the reservation, and in the world. The stock market tumbled, and thousands of natives and others rushed out to shout in personal panic holes on reservations. Others shouted into panic holes at reserved Tizzy Sites located near Fort Snelling, Minnehaha Park in Minneapolis, Saint Thomas College in Saint Paul, and the shoreline of the Mississippi river near the University of Minnesota.

Public and private institutions had dedicated specific panic sites, a more effective balance of fear, aversion, and resentment than drugs and the therapy cuts and clauses provided by mental health clinics. The earth shivered that night, and elected politicians were obliged to heave at least a pathetic moan of sympathy in response to the earthly rage of citizens over the grave economy and outset of the federal sectors of endorsements.

The Baron of Patronia, a great native healer, created the custom of shouting into panic holes more than a century ago on the west side of Bad Medicine Lake. He shouted into panic holes and the meadow turned blue with flowers, and he coached his children to heal the earth with wild shouts. Smart mongrels mimicked the healer and barked into panic holes and waited and waited for the sound of a return bark, woof, bellow, or bay. That original bark into a panic hole was heard around the world. The nearby meadows burst into glorious blues.

The Panic Hole Chancery, a continuation of the native custom of wild shouts, was founded a generation later in a faculty office in the Department of Native American Indian Studies at the University of Minnesota. Captain Shammer, the chairman of the department at the time, initiated original and popular native courses, and endorsed the training of irony dogs, the radical program of panic hole shouts, and encouraged the pirate native broadcasts of Panic Radio.

Gichi Noodin, the dutiful son of the native founder of Panic Radio, broadcast the voices of panic and stories of natural rage from secret locations on reservations and in cities. He drove a rusty blue van and reported wild shouts on the road, at urban reservations, parks, campsites, casinos, and from cardboard box precincts under bridges. Panic Radio was an elusive native station that broadcast free and without a license for more than forty years.

Captain Gichi Noodin traded his mottled blue pirate radio van two days after the congressional abrogation of treaties for a sleek pontoon houseboat, forty feet long with two solar outboard engines, and moored on Lac des Bois or Lake of the Woods.

The *Baron of Patronia* was christened in honor of the originator of wild shouts and panic holes. The houseboat was about the same length as the *canot de maître*, the Montréal fur trade canoes. Gichi Noodin painted great surges of waves on the cabin, deck, and freeboards of the houseboat, similar to the *Great Wave off Kanagawa* by Hokusai, and then he was ready to rescue the exiles and mongrels at a deserted dock near

Kakageesick Bay, named in honor of Everlasting Sky, a native healer who had lived for more than a hundred years on Muskeg Bay, Lake of the Woods.

The *Baron of Patronia* sailed in silence that first night and without navigation lights. Specter Drones and other monitors were restricted to the sectors, and the security agencies were not permitted to conduct surveillance over international waters, but satellite radio transmissions were recorded and scanned by electronic detectors.

Waasese created the laser holoscenes at night with advanced carbon nanosphere lithium anode batteries that stored power from small solar reactive cones. She provided the electronics and power to create marvelous laser shows and the popular nightly broadcast on Panic Radio.

Panic Radio broadcast the getaway stories of the exiles, a wild and ironic account of native survivance and liberty. Some of the nightly stories were related to selected articles of the constitution. Gichi Noodin teased the historical place name Northwest Angle and announced on Panic Radio that the name had been changed to the Angle of Liberty.

"Liberty with a slant," declared Justice Molly Crèche.

The Red Lake Reservation became a sector at the same time as the White Earth Nation, and that would include the conversion of the detached section of reservation treaty land at Northwest Angle. The surveillance on that remote sector was carried out with three miniature cameras on the dock, one light post, and the border station, but no monitors on the nearby islands near the international border.

The *Baron of Patronia* anchored the second night as a ruse at Bukete Island in Canada. Several days later, secure that our exile had been fully reported and documented outside of the United States, we sailed back over the border to Fort Saint Charles on Manidooke Minis, or the island of spiritual power, once named Magnuson's Island, near the Angle of Liberty in Lake of the Woods.

On October 22, 2034, we created a new literature of survivance in response to the abrogation of native treaties, reservations, and the constitution. That same day, and precisely three hundred years earlier, Pierre Gaultier de La Vérendrye had invited woodland natives to visit the new fur trade post at Fort Saint Charles.

La Vérendrye abandoned the new post a few years later when Jean Baptiste de La Vérendrye, his eldest son, Jean-Pierre Aulneau, the Jesuit mission priest, and nineteen exuberant voyageurs were murdered and beheaded on a nearby island of fur trade ghosts that was later named Massacre Island in Lake of the Woods.

The exiles created a sense of presence with overnight stories, the secure descendants of fur traders. We imagined a scene three months later on January 1, 1734, when the trader and his son Jean-Baptiste provided tobacco, bullets and gunflints, axes, awls, glass beads, and vermillion, the red mercury pigment to the natives on the island.

La Vérendrye, a prominent and ambitious fur trader, was a military officer in French Canada. He traded material objects, harvested wild rice and corn with natives, and he received in return beaver and other peltry.

That first night on the island we mourned the spirits of so many totemic animals slaughtered in the mighty rush of the fur trade. Justice Molly Crèche related a native song to honor the animal spirits at Fort Saint Charles on Manidooke Minis and on other islands in Lake of the Woods.

> dead beaver
> lost totems
> hear our names
> we grieve forever
> in the clouds

Fort Saint Charles became the strategic station of our exile and the new site of the constitution because of the extraordinary stories about the history of the native island. The fur trade fort was located less than a mile from the international border with Canada. We could easily sail over the border to avoid surveillance.

Moby Dick proposed several nightly radio stories on the international border. Scenes of the great novel of his nickname would have been a natural choice, an exotic white whale that heaves the waves on Lac des Bois, but instead he prepared several faraway scenes from *Winnetou: The Apache Knight*, an obscure, romantic, and chancy adventure by the nineteenth-century German novelist Karl May.

The heroic escapades of Old Shatterhand, the fantastic blood brother of Winnetou, the fictional Apache warrior, were read out loud in the melodramatic, ironic, and stagey voices of the eight exiled natives on Panic Radio.

Old Shatterhand rode a horse named Lightning.

Winnetou named his horse Wind.

Panic Radio broadcast every night that autumn on the international border of Lake of the Woods. The eight exiles envisioned on those marvelous nights a constitution of continental liberty that was in motion, and not restrained by the metes and bounds of any treaty. The exiles had recovered the spirit of the voyageurs and the natural motion of liberty.

Captain Gichi Noodin introduced Winnetou, the mythically correct, utopian native, secure with horses and nature, and the honorable German nicknamed Old Shatterhand, because of his mighty fists, that cloudy night on Panic Radio. The *Baron of Patronia* sailed at midnight with a full crew of exiles on the border and broadcast selections of the novel by Karl May.

Old Shatterhand related that "Winnetou had made an impression upon me such as I had never received from any other man. He was exactly my age, yet of greater parts, and this I felt from the first glance at him. The proud earnestness of his clear, velvety eyes, the quiet certainty of his bearing, and the profound sorrow of his fine young face had revealed it to me. How admirable had been his conduct and that of his father!"

Later, the exiles teased the references to "greater parts" and "velvety eyes," and continued the broadcast with tricky original stories about Old Wannabe, the mythical, plushy, likeable warrior of horny Norwegian farm boys in northern Wisconsin. Old Wannabe had a "certainty of his bearing," an enormous penis that once served as a natural rudder on the Great Lakes, and guided emigrant farmers to the great ports of paradise.

Gichi Noodin pretended that he was never certain which of the two mythical stories enchanted the listeners more, the sincere and "velvety eyes" of Winnetou, the Apache warrior, or the greater parts of Old Wannabe in the folk tales of the Norwindians.

2

MOBY DICK

The White Foxy Casino gamers and natives oldsters were naturally wary at times about new totems, and some teased me about the fishy names, but no one ever forgot the aquarium fish were my sacred totems.

The fish were exceptional and deserved the nicknames of great explorers because of the past abuses of deformities and totems. Truly everyone, humans, sandhill cranes, water ouzels, spiders, beavers, bears, bats, bobcats, coywolves, and goldfish were explorers, captains, sailors, and sometimes traders on solitary voyages in a strange world.

The White Foxy Casino was a strange world.

Chewy and the seven exiles were explorers at the same time, and we earned our nicknames on many expeditions, creation jaunts, and side stories, but humans were never considered totems to fish, animals, birds, or even the tricky spirits. The mongrels were curious and loyal scouts, and more sensitive to a meal, of course, than to the fancy of a totem. So, maybe natives were once the same as mongrels, loyalty to a totem and a meal, and nothing more but a wild manner, memories, a few good trickster stories, and sacred poses with tags of tradition.

The totemic eatery theme and deadly customs of the fur trade were converted by the eight exiles into original totemic associations that were plainly provided in the Constitution of the White Earth Nation. The exiles created new totems, not the usual heavy breath of bear, chase of deer, or moose stories over a wild dinner, and the exiles never told beaver, river otter, marten, or fox stories in the manly cast and commerce of the trade. Our heartfelt totems were secure in memory, original, personal, and visionary to a fault. The totemic creatures of the exiles were wolf spiders, bobcats, moccasin flowers, bats, coywolves, praying mantis, my deformed aquarium fish, and the mysterious river otter medicine bundle carried by Justice Molly Crèche.

Maybe only native shamans were secure enough in the treacherous natural world to tease the unnamable, the cues and jitters of nature with a visionary sway of silence and death, but not just the words. The old shamans sometimes restored spirits with obscure gestures and wild stories that were never the same, and with chancy visions could shy an animal or haunt a native game hunter with the slightest tease and trace of an ancient passion.

The Holy Rule of Saint Benedict was twice revised at the headwaters of the Mississippi River. Benedictine monks created the most original and erotic totemic unions with furry animals, and the association was not a totemic eatery, peltry trade, or tease of the sacred. The erotic unions were created with troubled cloisters not constitutions, and came to mind with thoughts about the migration of monks in the fifteenth century to the headwaters of the Mississippi River at Lake Itasca.

The Benedictine monks established a wild monastery near the headwaters named Fleury sur Gichiziibi. The monks were pious explorers in the red pines, truly exotic, the exiles of debauchery and monarchy, and devoted their entire time and tease to godly celibacy, until a native shaman at the headwaters more than four centuries ago distracted the monks with wild trickster stories about erotic animals. Some monks shivered with repressed ecstasy, of course, and then separated from the totems and stories, turned to absolute silence and meditation. The other more erotic monks masturbated with various animals and wrote about their carnal totemic connections with bears, rabbits, beaver, and other furry creatures.

The monks reasoned that the mere exercise of onanism with wild animals, an erotic totemic association, was not a sin, or wilt of holy spirits, because animals were created with no godly soul or sense of original sin, and never a cause of salvation. These dutiful monks created an explicit monastic manuscript, an original rescript of erotic touch, tease, and arousal with furry animals that enjoined but never violated the vows of celibacy.

The *Manabosho Curiosa* was discovered in a backstreet bookstore in

London. Pellegrine Treves, a rare book and document collector, had acquired the original parchment manuscript at auction more than a century ago. The erotic manuscript was read only by the selected friends of the collector, and reportedly was never released or published in any form.

Chewy Browne, my great-aunt, told me that she and other natives had read some of the erotic stories at Saint Benedict's Mission on the White Earth Reservation. Much later a copy of the original manuscript was uncovered in the library at Saint John's Abbey, a Benedictine Monastery in Minnesota. The monks allowed me to publish a limited edition of the *Manabosho Curiosa* because the erotic totemic scenes in the sole manuscript had aroused unruly stories and unwholesome activities in the monastic library.

The monks of the past and the exiles of the present shared and accepted at least two earthly notions, that the tease of animals and shamans was rampant, and incessant torments of revised native traditions and the miseries of modernism were relieved by the ordinary pleasures of masturbation. Some totemic monks, native storiers, and artists were always ahead of ordinary conventions and precepts, but onanism and the constitution were banished by the tradition fascists and sector governor.

The celibate monks who had shunned the shaman of the headwaters continued to obey a strict obedience to the holy precepts, the godly pose of monarchs, and vanished without a trace in the rush of winter. The totemic monks of wild masturbation with animals were in the erotic book, but not the book that separates mortals from natural teases and the faults of totems. The eight exiles had more in common with the totemic monks than the tradition fascists and sector governor. The stories were not the same but the animals and totemic unions were forever in the book. Maybe books were the earthly outcome of totems, the erotic scenes with furry animals, and the cruelty of the fur trade.

Godtwit Moon was anxious and red as a beet when he came close to the casino aquariums of deformed tropical fish, a reminder of the rare and unrepeatable tease of nature. Later he turned almost smoky blue when he learned that the *Manabosho Curiosa* was sold with floral beadwork, miniature birch bark canoes, foreign spirit catchers, carved walking sticks, and other native curios at the White Foxy Casino.

The sector governor was lonesome, and cruel at times, a piety poseur, and perverse, and mundane in that order of nuisance company. Yes, he befriended me at first and then banished me from the sector and reservation because of my totemic fish and absolute loyalty to the Constitution of the White Earth Nation.

The sector governor staged an outrage over the erotic stories at every event, and he seemed to focus his pious fury on the fantastic scenes of monks and opossums, and yet he boasted with no sense of irony about the delicious country flavor of redneck opossum stew that his mother made at home in Georgia, Alabama, and Kentucky. The name of his home state and maternal stew changed with the time and stories. Godtwit was born in Chicago, roamed with the raccoons in Los Angeles, and the only opossum stew he ever celebrated was served in prison.

Natives were sometimes shy but never starchy, not really, and the stories of the erotic monks with snowshoe hares and opossum were greatly embellished from the original monkish versions in the *Manabosho Curiosa*. The new grotesque stories were ironic, and the tradition fascists certainly would have banished the monks and the totemic animals for the practice of masturbation. The fascists actually removed the book from the casino and set out to silence the erotic totemic stories. These curbed natives of pious manners were the new sector accusers and hearsay gatekeepers of hazy sacred traditions.

Godtwit was an outcast and envious, a cast similar to the political mistrust and envy dominance of many federal agents with only an obscure trace of native ancestry. The steward of the casino slot machines, bars, and restaurants was not the same as the meddler agents, but the dominant manners were similar. Godtwit was backed with the same old rash of venal toadies and washout couriers of favor and entitlements when he was named the sector governor.

Godtwit paused at the aquariums several times a day when he first arrived at the casino. He touched the thick glass and waited for the explorers to nose the print of his blunt and reddish finger. Once he was truly enamored with the glorious fins, mouth, and easy motion of Jeanne Baret. The poseur pointed and burst into laughter, scared the fish, and distracted the nearby gamers over slot machines when he heard the name of the explorer.

Maybe he was sensitive for an instant, and the first blunt gesture to the explorer was clumsy, or his unusual attention to the deformed fish was nothing more than the wily curiosity of an outcast. His manner, however, turned suddenly from crude curiosity to despotism on the very day he was named the sector governor.

The new governor cursed the fancy explorers in the aquarium on his executive prowls around the casino, and he no longer mentioned me by name. The totemic associations of the deformed fish in the aquarium were terminated with sector governance.

Godtwit was actually poisoned earlier, hours before the dance in the red pine, and already close to death at the time he was crushed under the tracks of a snow machine. The sector coroner reported that the poison had been consumed several hours before the governor had arrived with the Peace Hookers. The Debwe Heart Dance was not the cause of death on the shore of Many Point Lake.

Waaban Blue Union was not poison and was not the cause of his death. The blue luminous narcotic might have delayed the deadly effects of the actual poison, a noxious tablet of Deadly Nightshade, fabricated to resemble the standard prescription for high blood pressure. Someone placed one or more poison tablets in his pocket medicine container.

Godtwit had ranted about the reliability of the drugs for his heart and only trusted prescriptions prepared at Saint Cloud La Maison de Torture Extraordinaire. That one special prescription was truly extraordinary and terminal, and the sector security service commenced an investigation of the rendition dispensary.

The Manidoo Singers slowly circled the hardboard casket of Godtwit Moon. The singers vowed to honor the memory of the native dead with traditional songs, hymns, and stories to encourage the spirit to enter the other native world, and not to haunt the survivors. That ceremony for the sector demon, poisoned and crushed to death under the tracks of a snow machine, should have been songs of soul separation and castaway spirits, but the ordinary gestures and customary solemnity were distracted by moans, teases, and cagey derision of the dead governor.

Chewy, my great-aunt, had been a dedicated singer for more than sixty years, and she could rouse stray spirits with a marvelous soprano voice, an inescapable rich timbre and mood of mercy. The only other native mourners at the grave that cold morning were his enemies.

Naturally the exiles hated the sector governor, cursed his name and presence, and then saluted his absence. We were at the grave to be sure his body was actually buried, and his nasty spirit was forever exiled from the world, or any domain. Not even the ice woman would bother to tease the mean spirit of the governor. We sang along loudly, an operatic mockery, because there was no greater desolation than to be separated with derision in the spirit world, and then the exiles waited to hear the last cold shovel of backfill at the grave.

The murder of the sector governor would not change the autocratic order of our banishment because we refused to renounce the Constitution of the White Earth Nation. The seven exiles and my great-aunt were dedicated to carry out the virtue and integrity of the democratic constitution in exile at Fort Saint Charles on Lake of the Woods.

Godtwit swore, muttered, and bedeviled the deformed fish every time he came near the two aquariums at the White Foxy Casino. He despised the very sight of any disability, double dorsal fins, or a minor speech hesitation, and loathed my distorted and humpbacked fish, each one named in honor of a great explorer, Marco Polo, Juan de Fuca, Jeanne Baret, Sir Walter Raleigh, Francis Drake, Amerigo Vespucci, Vasco da Gama, Christopher Columbus, Matteo Ricci, and the father, brother, emissary, and dressy seventeenth-century mariner of mappery in New France, Samuel de Champlain.

Godtwit cut the electrical power to the two aquariums a few days after he was named sector governor. The gamers that night were obsessed with the electronic animals, fruit, and other scenes on the slot machines and never noticed the gasps and yawns of the fish, or deathly bumps on the dark glass. The great explorers expired overnight in the stagnant water, and in the early morning Christopher Columbus floated on the surface of the dark aquarium, a deformed angelfish with four feathery pelvic fins nibbled away by the other frantic fish.

My special totemic fish were separated in two huge aquariums, one with gorgeous vegetation, and the other with castles, caverns, tunnels, and many places to hide. Juan de Fuca was a tiger barb, actually six of them, and they were numbered and easily identified by the singular shapes. The other fish had distorted mouths, some with three eyes, crooked spines, twisted humps, gnarled bellies, double, triple, and more fins, and other incomparable exotic shapes and comic features.

Matteo Ricci, a clown barb with stunted pelvic fins, was very active, and bright, but not that dreadful morning of his slow death. His twisted nostrils were silent at the surface of the dark aquarium.

Jeanne Baret, a marvelous goldfish with a giant mouth and five dorsal fins, shimmered to death through the waves of plants in the aquarium. She was much more curious than the other explorers, and even teased the elders close to the glass, but the late-night gamers were oblivious to the last feathery waves and turns of frantic fancy. Many of the gamers were connected to oxygen tanks, but not the totemic explorers in the two aquariums.

Samuel de Champlain, a betta fish with glorious waves of double soft ray fins, was overturned and floated with an incredible serenity. I reached into the water that morning and touched his bright wispy fins.

Marco Polo was named a firemouth fish with a bright red mouth, a moody swimmer, and that morning his mouth was wide and dead on the thick surface of the aquarium. Amerigo Vespucci was a black molly explorer dead at the bottom of the aquarium sea. Sir Walter Raleigh was a bleeding heart tetra, hidden and dead in an aquarium cavern. Sir Francis Drake was named a marbled hatchetfish with two enormous goggled eyes, and he must have tried many times to jump out of the dark tank of death. Vasco da Gama was a livebearer platy fish, reddish with two rows of dark dorsal fins, and a double humped forehead.

My totems were terminated that night, three centuries after the beaver and other animals were slaughtered in the empire fur trade. My totem of crippled aquarium fish had no value in any trade, but the sector governor used his new power to execute the explorers.

The deformed fish were totemic explorers in casino aquariums, a new reservation of exceptional creatures. The tropical fish traders heard stories about my totem and sent the contorted aquarium fish to me at no cost, otherwise the faulty fish would have been terminated as unsalable. They were tropical migrants and deserved the nicknames of great explorers.

The gamers praised my totems, and at the same time teased me over the strange collection of deserted creatures captured in the two aquariums. Some natives were moved to laughter and tears as the fish nosed the thick glass of the aquariums. My totemic fish might have thought the same about the crippled gamers, the many elders with walkers, canes, and oxygen masks.

Naturally, my totem became the subject of cruel and sympathetic stories, and the gestures were never clear to me because even my family and close friends would secretly abandon deformed creatures, birds, mice, voles, mongrels, snakes, turtles, and anything with one eye, too many eyes, ears, or a missing foot or paw, in a horse trough near my cabin at Bad Boy Lake.

Archive was clearly secretive about Henry Badge, his lover for several years, and the second sector governor. Henry was eager and smarmy in her pursuit of artists and people in positions of authority, and Archive was a showy writer bedeviled by the wild sex, and many encounters were in public places. They humped two or three times between the aquariums at the casino, and teased me that they only wanted to arouse the deformed fish. Henry raised her summer dress and pressed her sturdy cheeks on the thick glass, an incredible magnification in my view on the other side of the aquarium. Christopher Columbus and Jeanne Baret were aroused enough to nose the print of her sweaty body. The late-night gamers never heard the slightest sighs or hurried murmurs near the aquariums.

Henry was her birth name, not a nickname, but maybe it was a mistake. Faith, her mother, rejected the girly names, and her father was a federal police officer and seldom at home. Most men, natives or not, overstated the scuttlebutt of her lusty moves, but not by me, and my stories were never about the aquarium encounter. Henry had served as a sergeant in the army, and some veterans concocted erotic stories about her time in the Middle East.

Henry had returned to the reservation about the same time that Godtwit was paroled as the overseer of casino slot machines and restaurants. Henry was hired as a security agent. At first she was warmhearted about the fish, and me, but later she turned cautious, very distant, and would not show her sympathies.

Archive never mentioned that Henry became a crony, confidante, and the executive assistant to Godtwit the same week he was named the sector governor. Henry might have been bewitched because she never told me why she refused to intervene to save the explorers, my totems. So, maybe she was the one who poisoned the nasty rendition parolee, only to become the second governor.

Moby Dick has been my nickname since my first and only theatrical performance as a child, one of three natives, and we were the source of motion in a huge papier-mâché white whale on stage at the public school. I was at the great head of the white whale, and thrashed about with such magical force that the body broke into three parts. The papier-mâché head continued to move on stage, and even more with the caution of the teachers and the cheers of the audience.

Some of my relatives were convinced that my totemic associations with deformed fish started with my childhood role as the grotesque head of the great white whale. Chewy borrowed a copy of *Moby-Dick* from the library and read the incredible stories of Ishmael and the white whale to me at night. My native nickname was a tease that became a cue of crippled fish and great literature.

The Manidoo Singers circled the tiny ornate casket of the dead totemic aquarium explorers, and they sang native dream songs of the seasons, and traditional honoring songs to reach the spirits and great guardians of the deformed fish.

> *With a large bird, above me*
> *I am walking in the sky*
> *I entrust myself to the wind*
>
> *Let us stand, to see my body*
> *As I would like to be seen*

Christopher Columbus, Matteo Ricci, Jeanne Baret, Marco Polo, Samuel de Champlain, Sir Walter Raleigh, and the other great aquarium explorers were buried outback near my cabin at Bad Boy Lake.

Chewy earned her nickname only because she chewed paper, a practice she inherited from distant relatives in the fur trade. The French, she told me, chewed paper, and that was the meaning of papier-mâché. She was moved to tears at the tiny gravesite, and chanted twice the names of each and every dead explorer.

My great-aunt took care of me when my mother died in an automobile accident, and tried to protect me in a world of nasty taunts. She taught me to nurture other creatures, and especially the many chickens that she taught to dance, how to survive native teases, and how to outwit my enemies, but there was no way to overcome the demonic presence of the sector governor with wit, pity, or mockery.

Chewy was determined to be an exile and packed two duffel bags to escape that cold autumn night with the seven exiles on the *Baron of Patronia*. She brushed aside any praise of a great soprano voice and spirit, and demanded that she be included with the exiles of liberty. I strongly supported my great-aunt, who was a wise delegate at the conventions and dedicated to the constitution, but the other exiles had decided not to allow her to leave the sector. Chewy was diabetic and she needed drugs and the direct treatment provided by the new sector medical center at the Coy Care Casino.

The nomination of my great-aunt to serve only with the reserve exiles was clearly condescending. Yet, more than a hundred other older natives had accepted the reserve stature as exiles, and stayed close to the slot machine exiles, but my great-aunt shouted back that actual exile was the only serious act of native survival, not medical care at the casino. Chewy was never discouraged, so she persuaded a niece to secretly follow the exiles by car to the remote dock that night near Warroad on Lake of the Woods.

John Kakageesick, or *gaagige giizhig*, forever sky or day in translation, lived as a hunter and healer on the shore of Muskeg Bay in Warroad, Minnesota, for more than a hundred years. Gichi Noodin selected a remote dock near the original federal land allotment of Kakageesick on the Warroad River. Our exile started at that memorable dock, a new native liberty.

Everlasting Sky died in Warroad on December 6, 1968, at an estimated age of 124, and that small town honored the native who had lived on

Muskeg Bay and Lake of the Woods fourteen years before Minnesota was admitted to the Union as a state, and he was sixteen years old when Abraham Lincoln was elected president of the United States.

Archive told a story about his great-uncle Clément Beaulieu who was a journalist for the *Minneapolis Tribune* at the time. Beaulieu attended and wrote about the native ceremony and public funeral of Everlasting Sky. Daniel Raincloud, the *midewiwin* spiritual leader, honored the native spirit of *gaagige giiizhig* in an ironic space, a public school gymnasium. Raincloud jiggled a small rattle over a medicine bundle, placed red gloves and tobacco in the coffin, and the presence of that sound has lasted forever on Lake of the Woods.

Chewy chanted an honoring song, slowly waved and danced down the rickety dock as she towed two duffel bags of clothes, chicken feed, and diabetic drugs, and reported for duty as an exile.

Nine exotic chickens, two Rhode Island Red, three Dorking, two Plymouth Rock, and two Indian Game chickens danced with my great-aunt down the dock, slight body turns one way and then the other, toes and claws forward, and then back with a perfectly timed sough, cluck, and soprano chant.

Captain Gichi Noodin shouted out the name of my great-aunt as an honorable member of the exiled crew of liberty. The other exiles chanted in unison and then waited for the spunky chickens to dance and bounce on board the *Baron of Patronia*.

Mother Teresa and Sardine were shied by the fancy chickens and nosed my great-aunt down the dock. The other mongrels pushed at the duffel bags, and White Favor whistled with ecstasy. Only a sector savage could have resisted the healers, the sway and pirouette of the chickens, the manner, humor, and natural celebration of the mongrels.

Chewy was born an exile, she matured as an exile, chewed papier-mâché as an exile, and raised me as an exile with the chickens, and she could never survive as a sector prisoner with oxygen, a fancy wheelchair, and ready slot machines at the renamed Coy Care Casino.

Archive, Savage Love, Justice Molly Crèche, and the other exiles returned to the dock and mocked the dance moves of my great-aunt, a mighty tease of devotion, and the chickens and mongrels gathered in the great show.

Chewy was in her nineties, and that cold night on the rickety dock we named my great-aunt the senior exiled soprano of liberty and great chicken maestro of the White Earth Nation. She raised her hands, nine chickens at her side, swayed with the mongrels, and told stories to honor Clément Beaulieu who actually wrote the Constitution of the White Earth Nation.

Chewy was determined to escape the nasty politics of the sector and converted medical care center in the Coy Care Casino. She was weary that so many distant native relatives had capitulated to the sector management and yet continued to depend on her to care for their children day and night, but never had the time to hear a story of native liberty. She was a mighty singer, a great native healer, and storier of natural motion. The sector toadies taunted my great-aunt because she had absolute faith in a democratic constitution and native continental liberty.

Chewy sang an honoring song in a slow and evocative soprano voice, *brave warriors, where have you gone, ho kwi ho ho*, and a dream song in honor of *naanabozho*, the trickster in native stories, *dance and sing across the water, if you open your eyes they will turn red*, as the *Baron of Patronia* silently moved away from the dock into Muskeg Bay. My great-aunt wore a blue Treaty Shirt decorated with bright beaded flowers and the giveaway stains of twenty years since the ratification of the Constitution of the White Earth Nation.

At dawn the next morning the *Baron of Patronia* slowly cruised on calm waters across the international border, and everyone was on deck for that moment, the natural motion of exile and continental liberty. The mongrels touched, bumped, and wagged at the bow, and the chickens clucked and bounded down the deck and over the great waves painted on the cabin.

Chewy stood on deck with the mongrels and chanted the native names of the four seasons to the serene music of *Spiegel im Spiegel*, mirror in the mirror, by the Estonian composer Arvo Pärt. The transcendent tones of her soprano voice and the meditative sounds of the piano and violin broadcast on Panic Radio were a harmonious union of natural motion and traces of the seasons. Chewy created the mood of seasons with the tone of her voice, the music of exiles, a touch of winter in the autumn, and great clouds of summer in the memories of the spring.

dagwaagin autumn
biboon winter
ziigwan spring
niibin summer

Captain Gichi Noodin of the *Baron of Patronia* was the most familiar voice of Panic Radio and he had arranged the broadcast of that significant moment of liberty and emotive music on the international border of Lake of the Woods.

3
SAVAGE LOVE

Name me a native exile, but not with ordinary words, not suicide similes, not with pushy adjectives over the brink of meaning. I am an exile and write to an absence, not to the cultural nostalgia of a presence, not to some sentimental reminiscence of shamans or natural words, and never to editors or grace favors. I write to eight native exiles never fairly named in archives and libraries.

I was born in exile, and stay in exile.

Exile is my natural motion.

Names can name no lasting names, a paradox ascribed to Lao Tzu and the *Tao Te Ching*, or the ironic contradiction that the many names of natives never lasted. Natives were named in discovery, named in conversions, in mission and federal schools, renamed over and over again in histories, and the exiles without a name endure with the anomalies of nicknames.

Nicknames were stories of motion not presence.

My words were an absolute native absence, and never named a presence. The pretense of presence ran wild with delusions, and once was considered a tease in trickster stories, the tease and wit of provocation, or the grudges of irony. The nostalgia and literary romance of presence, the pokey of presence, would hardly continue in my name, or with these words of my absence. Native names were exiled in a hoax of presence, and the deceptions were moody and ironic.

The ancient words were almost dead on arrival in the woodland, and the high and mighty missionaries reined back native visions. Yes, the churchy words were cut and run in translation, a new rendition, and with no seasons of irony. The treaty words were disabled, dead and buried outback with the bloody nouns of liberty.

Rightly worried, lonesome readers turn over the same order of words dead on the page and stage. Presence must wait at the elbow of every reader to be revealed in some subject, or the fakery of an object, and the righteous words must at least deliver the shadows of presence, or a better ghost or totem to bear our nicknames.

I write to silence, to the end of language, to the dead, not to the book. I am in the book, not the object, and write only to evade the nostalgia of native traditions, the teases and hesitations of the moment, to beset the hokey promises of urgent words, the hoodwinkers of the now, and to escape the sinister now for the obvious reasons that natives ran out of traditions and stories more than three centuries ago with the fur trade, the many, many diseases, and the bad breath of missionaries.

The romance of that native moment, the natural native now, was a deception, not a presence, and not a now, never now, now, say now. Poseurs and the lonesome couriers of the words might never endure the contrived treasure troves of the now moment.

Trace the now as empty. That wordy entrance to a sense of presence was the deception of tradition, turn around and the entrance has vanished, not a trace of the entry to the now. Natives were never more than exiles and must write in the past tense, write to an absence.

My words were not the tease of silence or some race to an original moment of the past. No one can remember the past names, stories of the past, or native origins. The next stories were the origins, but natives were not the outright origins, not the delivery notice of muskrats or monotheism.

The origin stories of tricksters were high water nostalgia for the absence of the earth. No one, no poets, no shamans, no artists ever heard the original chant to soar, the creation set to swim, or held the evolutionary strings of that great kite of native traditions. The promises of the past ganged up on absence, ganged up on the overnight boredom of shamanic hoaxers, and became high feigns of presence and concocted originality.

The words of our denatured democratic governance were never about the now, no one would dare to ratify the now, only the distance of meaning was drafted, so abstract in concept that the absence rode high in the cockpit of the preamble and every article of the Constitution of the White Earth Nation.

The constitution was never a presence, only a collection of promissory notes and abstract articles, but those ratified egalitarian words have always been an absence, beholden to the territorial borders and jurisdiction provided by the treaty of 1867, and continued with the plenary power favors of the United States Congress.

The abrogation of the constitution was the start, not the end, not the absence and not the creation of a fake presence. The actual story of the constitution started with termination, the abrogation, not the delegate ratification or referendum by native citizens. The forty sworn delegates at the four conventions created a fugitive constitution, only the articles of native motion, and the delusion of a secure presence, but notions of the here and now passed with humor and the free meals. The actual story of the constitution started with the exiles.

Yet, the elusive words of absence in the constitution were worth the bother, worth the delusions, and worth the poses of the now, worthy at least until some greater absence overcomes the conceit of the words and articles. That premier notion of continental liberty in the preamble of the constitution was created as the evasion of the now, the escape of the tedious civics of the now, the political absence of the gist and action of now and liberty.

Liberty was nostalgia, never the moment.

We, so named *we*, the pronoun poseur *we*, the exiles in natural motion on cold water, we cruise on national borders, as we once cruised the boundaries of creation and federal treaties, and we were named the exiles of liberty. The exiles became the purse of native liberty.

Pronouns were borrowed with no sense of person or presence, no second nature of first, second, or third person in the past tense. Only the fourth person created a sense of an elusive presence in stories. Pronouns deceived readers, no *me*, no *you*, no *he*, *she*, or *them*, but then who cared or carried on the stories? Right, social media, network blogs, and the pronoun demons of gossip theory.

The word *exile* was inscrutable, the tease of ordinary banishment, an absence, not a presence, and the actual pronouncements of our exile were ironic, because there were no exiles of that notion of presence named liberty. *Exile* was a courier word, a breakaway from cultural simulations. The politics of entitlements were always ironic in native stories, the fount of ancestors, ironic in gestures of presence, and in the steady pretense of cultural memory.

These words, the silence and absence of these words, were my only publication. Archive directed me to write, and to honor the absence of the constitution, our exile, and these words of absence landed in the book, *Treaty Shirts*, but not now, never now, never at the moment.

My exile was a fugitive pose, and this autocritical essay was a venture, not a structure, a contention, a resistance, never a tradition, and my essay was more trickster story than native exposition of exile or the winsome and ironic declaration of natural motion and continental liberty.

These native essays were a declaration of absence, the start of the story, not the end, not a literary lament. The exiles resisted the new sectors, the new synthetic narcotics, the black teeth of tradition dancers, and the concocted notion that our exile was a revolution. The exiles were naturals at wordplay, the tease of reason, contingencies and ideologies, and the ironic demise of final vocabularies in the spirit of the philosopher Richard Rorty.

Archive deftly conveyed that our exile was a presence, a moment of actuality, and yet he never truly simulated the nostalgia of presence over absence, or the pinch of now, that elusive aura of existence. Exile was not a choice of presence, or absence, never a now of eight native expatriates. We were the storiers of exile, not the presence or the now or political expatriation.

These words were the tease of now, not the presence, and only the ephemeral appearance of the moment. The exiles were an absence, and the now was underwater, in the natural waves and ancient stone, and the stories of a native presence were in the stones of trickster stories. The stones wait to burst apart in campsite fires.

Archive knew we might never survive the winter on Lake of the Woods. Fort Saint Charles was never a native commune or presence, only a crude moment in the rush of the fur trade, one more colonial enterprise, and remained a concocted absence of continental liberty. The exiles were the prey of winter, similar to the celibate and exiled monks without an animal to stimulate, only mongrels, chickens, and the unruly words of our exile, and our absolute absence. Natives have always been the prey of cozy traditions and the lousy now of treaties and the endorsement sector.

Exile doubles the evasion of the now.

No worries, none, because my last word was silence, not the words in the book. My words of absence have no native memory that would turn me into a story. I resist the tease of now, the literary toggles of the now, the fakery of now, the fusions of now as much as futurity.

My absence runs with the mongrels, with a bump and whistle, an instant pant and pose of presence, the loyal touch and heal of a wet nose, but not that memorable now, the big now of native shamans, hairy visions, or the great presence of the seductive ice woman beyond the pale of winter.

The mongrels were in the book only as the nostalgia of their presence and loyalty. The mongrels bay and bark and were the absolute absence of some tricky eternity. That wild sound of absence and irony could be my only story.

Desperate natives turned that sense of absence over to the spirit fakers, shamans of the now and then, and finally left their hearts out to dry with the missionaries of the moment and eternity, and their totems out for the voyageurs of the fur trade, the ironic stories of presence out for the commerce of ethnography. The curators at museums and universities convened the simulations of that silence at the start of the seasons, the natural motion of stories, and creative images on stone and leather, canvas, and paper. Native creative art became an absence in the museums.

Now, the ever modernist now, waits around with no spirit or heart of native stories. Native spirits have always been an absence, the heart of tradition a prison, and bodies have been weighted down with centuries of sugar, fry bread, salt pork, and the bad food of the now and civilization.

The pretense of now was absolute in native casinos, and the gamers played to the now, now or never. The trivial tease of natives on skateboards became a more memorable scene of originality. So many native doctorates of the now, the sacred academic now, doctorates of presence with heavy sources from the pale of libraries, and then turned back to nurture a fake now of casino virtue, employment, and the literature of victimry.

There were too many ceremonies and heart dances to keep track of the fake healers. So, some natives turned back to the mongrels, to our oldest companions of absence on the road, the teasers and healers with a better nose for sources of sex, food, and the absence of irony.

White Favor and Sardine never pointed to the now, or ran with the empty words of presence. Mongrels run on the margins of absence, only the sleeve dogs favor a stake in the fakery of now and a presence, a pedigree now in the games away from home.

So, who can create an original native story? Maybe the natives on skateboards were the new tricksters of absence, or the risky now timers with stained teeth, the ones who traded the desperate duties of the now for the ecstasy of untraceable synthetic narcotics.

Yes, of course, the tease of now was our escape, as it has been since the very first contrary natives survived the severe winter and returned in the spring with inscrutable visions, songs, and elusive stories. Even then the notion of a native presence was no more than a season at a time.

The coywolf was my totem, a creature of absence as a descendant of wolves and coyotes. The name coywolf was a double absence, a natural resistance to the now, to presence, to the academic delusions of pure and true creatures. The coywolf has become my absence in a totemic name, and an eternal trace of absence, not presence.

"Where now? Who now? When now?"

These three queries, these words, the absence of my voice, the clauses of my literary absence, and the past tense must start with uncertainty, mockery of presence, the tease of now, and the eternal silence of words in the book. Tease the unnamable in the *The Unnamable* by Samuel Beckett, my favored book of ironic words of prey. He wrote, "I, say I. Unbelieving. Question, hypotheses, call them that. Keep going, going on, call that going, call that on."

So, call this going, going on with an exile soliloquy, unnamable, and an absence, unbelieving. My nickname now, my steady tease of treaties and governance now, and my exile of absence.

Treaty now? Sector now? Exile now?

The chickens danced, mongrels nosed the night air, and the music was haunting over the cold water, an exile scene but not the now or a presence, nothing now but our absence as exiles on Lake of the Woods.

Samuel Beckett was a partisan of ironic actualities, a native shaman of the unnamable, the master of silence and slivers of words, the disguises of color and meaning, and the elusive tease of resurrection and enlightenment. Beckett told Raymond Federman "it is worse not to write than to write," shortly before his death about fifty years ago in Paris.

Beckett might have declared that gossip theories were as memorable as rush hour trade and traffic. Hearsay was broadcast at every intersection, count the cultures, mothers, brothers, sisters, teachers, shamans, bartenders, bankers, and doctor scouts caught in the rush hour of hearsay, and with no turns to escape the crude scuttlebutt theorists of the past and ethnology.

I write to an absence, to the actualities of an absence, not now, not the now, never a presence, and my stories were unnamable and unpublished. Beckett delivered his literary mockery to publishers, and tormented the readers with an elusive gesture to the absence of meaning, the fake scent of meaning, but he teased the absence of actuality, the images of words, pronouns, and the trite favors of now.

Samuel Beckett travels with me, but not now.

Beckett had nothing to say about the now, he said so, words were exiled in an equivocal now, the now words of the subject, but there never was a subject to name the now. The word exile has been out, nothing more than an absence since Dante Alighieri, Alfred Dreyfus, Oscar Wilde, Émile Zola, Marc Chagall, Sigmund Freud, Lion Feuchtwanger, Pablo Neruda, Albert Camus, and Samuel Beckett.

Lake of the Woods became our new empire of absence and continental liberty. The dominion was overstated, but certainly an empire of necessary delusions when the federal treaty of our constitution and sovereignty was outsourced to a turnkey sector, and we were deported, mere pronouns of a national political ruse, exiled with a broadside on the water, counted out by clauses, the crack and crease of clauses, the means handed down by clauses, and nothing more critical or ironic that morning than the ruins of sector commerce and the native nostalgia of an empire war.

Archive taunted the toadies of the sector and declared our exile a second totemic empire war. Yes, the first totemic war was the fur trade. Three centuries later eight exiled natives were afloat, armed with an anthology of political delusions and resistance words, tricky stories, clauses, a solar powered houseboat, laser prominence, nightly panic broadcasts, nine chickens and five irony mongrels that avoid the now in a perfect cluck and lick and tease of presence. The second totemic empire war was with the sector cringers, toadies, tradition fascists, and the privileged parolees of *Rendition de Gentillesse* entrusted with the distribution of federal sector resources.

Native novelists ought to tease the latest visionaries, the strict conventioneers, the mighty shamans of shame and the raw, consorts and grievers over the abuse of natural motion, and that vital tease and uneasy sway of liberty. The wild and evocative native writers breached the truce with ordinary words, overturned the masters of precedence, chased the transience of seasons, shouted out loud to the clouds, turned away the totemic unions of nostalgia, and created ironic stories over the mortal set of monotheism and the summer graze of enlightenment. The literary cringers and casino lackeys waited and witnessed the outcome of late-night courses on the now.

Samuel Beckett cracked the enlightenment and tricky truce of words with double teases. The cracks exposed the collusion of poseurs, literary, cultural, and commercial, but once again the shamans of presence were decorated with cedar and sage, and the necessary stage of mockery and irony was conveyed to the casino gamers of the restated now, and to the electronic visions of the moment.

The great teases of the heart were in nature, not set in books, not in diamonds or traded at pawnshops, or in the rave of academics. The eight exiles were in the book, forever teased in the book *Treaty Shirts*. My firsthand words were a pitch and tease of absence, a provocation of the now and native nostalgia, the unrevealed scenery of now, and the counter ceremonials of exiles. My words were the runaways of presence and the truants of the now. These words of mine, and the tricky scenes were my first publication, by exile and chance of absence, not by choice.

Exile was never a now, never an actuality, or even a simulation of authenticity. The stories of exiles started at the end, not with portraits, surreal expressions, or conveyed in the ordinary tone of traditions. Our experiences of the constitution cannot be depicted as a native state or entreaty, and the short clumsy clauses of cultural memory and history were rightly overturned by irony, mockery, and my teases of absence. The sector governor and sentries were the eavesdroppers and misery-mongers of a treacherous casino culture.

Truly my stories were an absence, nothing, and started at the end of presence, yet my words were printed and bound in a book for eternity. We were in the book, forever, you, and me, the five mongrels of irony, nine fancy chickens, agents and envoys, the dead governor, surveillance sentries, sector minions of the casino now, and eight exiles of liberty.

No one has come closer to that woeful threshold, that turnstile of emptiness, and the absolute dead motion of printed words, the nostalgia of naturalism, than a native novelist. Maybe a literary shaman on the rebound from abuses of the sacred, or a sly getaway of contrition was closer to the traces of dead voices in the book.

The first native words were an absence, not a creation, and at a time without silence, a rage of gestures, and then the whispers and shouts of abstract names. The native rage of absence was overcome with tricky words of salvation and enlightenment, the pure reason of presence, and the absence of now in stories became the mighty slights of monarchies.

Patrick Henry never published that repeated phrase, "Give me liberty or give me death." No, these words were not exiled in print and then shouted out later as cultural slogans. The words of liberty and death were in the air and broke the silence of mundane politics, and changed the season that year, but never created a now or presence. "Give me liberty or give me death" was the ironic tease of a master storier, and he was wise not to have turned the sound of his voice, and gestures of an audience, into a precious moment, or dead voices in the book.

Patrick Henry never intended to write and publish the phrase, the dead voices. Yet, some readers have created the scene, the intense and ironic play of his voice that gave the words new meaning, the mirage of a moment, but there was no moment or now of liberty that we agreed with that cold and clear morning of exile on the international border of Lake of the Woods.

The mongrel healers were at my side, and perceived by scent and gestures, the irony of silence. The five mongrels trained with me and were naturals at detection, and barked at the absence of irony in the pretense of sector governance, and barked in harmony over *Rendition de Gentillesse* and the conversion of the White Foxy Casino to the Coy Care Casino. The mongrels never barked at the nightly holoscenes or at our stories of exile, but Mutiny, Wild Rice, and Sardine had started to wheeze, a whistle, and a noisy mongrel sway over the notions of now and presence. The wheeze was a distinct tone of mockery.

Sardine cocked her ear to the sound of waves.

Mother Teresa was a teaser extraordinaire, a coy healer of the now, and she shivered over the mere scent of worried hearts. Godtwit Moon, the dead governor, might have been healed with a nosy bump and shiver of Mother Teresa, and put right out of the fantasy of the now by a more direct and new perceptive sense of *Rendition de Gentillesse* than the mushy conventions of great moments of cultural presence at La Maison de Torture Extraordinaire.

White Favor was also a master teaser of the now, the absence of irony, and the fugitive meaning of words. He barked at the absence of irony, of course, and whistles with pleasure at the absence of meaning. The perception of dead words and voices deserved more than an ordinary mongrel moan, and more than a decent bark over the absence of irony.

White Favor lived with me for more than ten years, a stray mongrel related to the original and memorable White Dog who served Melvin McCosh, the tricky and eccentric owner of a bookstore more than seventy years ago near the University of Minnesota in Minneapolis.

McCosh taught the senior White Dog to fetch books by title from the bookstore shelves, and the booksy mongrel was rarely sidetracked with obscure subjects. The mongrel trotted and wagged directly to the correct section, history, literature, religion, and pawed the book, but he could not reach above the fourth level of shelves. White Dog pranced and barked for assistance to reach books on higher shelves. McCosh was a gentle teaser, and told me that the wartime comfort dogs were the ancestors of White Dog.

White Favor, the irony mongrel in exile, was a direct descendant of the clever mongrels loyal to readers and bookstore owners. Many generations later, the mongrel perception and selection of book titles included printed words, a natural scent and critical consciousness of empty words, feigned words, and dead voices in books. The mongrel whistles were a clear commentary on absence and the dummy runs of literacy.

White Favor never moaned but smartly whistled his way through the vacant words and dead voices of arrogant politicians, managers, academics, casino gamers, and federal agents, and at times barked and whistled at the same words, and always at heavy moments of the now. Some of his very best whistles were over selected books in libraries. White Favor bounded between the stacks of native literature and whistled a lucky tune.

Sylvia Beach, a suitable nickname, was the principal librarian at the William Warren Community College Library on the White Earth Nation, and she acquired an impressive collection of first edition books by native authors. Sylvia had a steady strut on narrow feet, and she wore heavy white socks and black sandals in summer and winter.

White Favor was her favored mongrel, a brilliant literary critic. She raved about his determined trot and whistle over books that were later designated for removal from the main shelves of the library. The mongrel trotted to the library at least once a week in the early years of the constitutional government, roamed and pranced between the stacks and whistled over the hardbound copies of *Hanta Yo* by Ruth Beebe Hill, *The Primal Mind: Vision and Reality in Indian America* by Jamake Highwater, *Education of Little Tree* by Forrest Carter, *Ind'n Humor* by Kenneth Lincoln, *The Blood Runs Like a River Through My Dreams* by Nasdijj, and he expressly barked and whistled many times over *The Divine Sex and Science of Vine Deloria* by Margo Rain Manypenny. White Favor whistled three notes based on "Paperback Writer" by The Beatles.

White Favor never barked, moaned, or whistled over the *Manabosho Curiosa*, a rare and censored manuscript that was first published by Moby Dick in a limited edition with fore edge decorations, or over the contentious and erotic novel *Bearheart: The Heirship Chronicles* by Gerald Vizenor. Sylvia Beach had secured several copies of both ironic and erotic books, the ancient stories of erotic monks and animals, and

the furious futurity stories of native catastrophe, but the righteous connivers borrowed and burned every copy of the two books. Sylvia Beach
continued to acquire new copies for the library. The last shelved copy
of *Bearheart* was removed and tortured to death a few months ago by
tradition fascists in an extreme moment of strange cultural nostalgia
and the sentiments of the sector now, now, now.

4

GICHI NOODIN

Panic Radio has broadcast without a license at least three hours every night for more than forty years. The first broadcasts were from a rusty blue van parked near colleges and universities, and from cardboard shadow cities under the interstate bridges in the city. The live broadcasts have continued on the international border in a houseboat named the *Baron of Patronia*.

The Baron of Patronia was the name of my great-uncle and, you know the story, he shouted and waved at bears and missionaries but never changed the weather or literature until he created the first panic holes and roared into the stony earth. The actual location of that maiden shout was a blue meadow near Bad Medicine Lake.

Natives were healed over the panic holes, and there were no dues or duties to the wily shamans, or recitations to the priestly hustle and bustle of salvation. Needless to say the old enterprise healers conspired to shame and shut down the panic holes, but the shouters gathered in the hundreds at country meadows and city parks and bellowed out the very names and venture cures of the doctors and politicians over personal and communal burrows of recovery.

The Baron of Patronia encouraged panic shouters in the ruins of civilization, and saluted once or twice a week the native woman who roared over a cardboard box with such musical vitality the range of her roars and shouts became regular recitals in the shadows of the highrise towers and interstate bridges, an overnight remedy of city misery.

Captain Shammer, my cousin, was raised with three sisters, two brothers, and seven mongrels on the Red Lust, a houseboat on Lake Itasca. He inherited the captaincy from his father Eighty, a nickname related to the atomic number of mercury. Shammer shouted into the summer waves, the first native since the fur trade to practice panic holes in natural motion on water, and he was haunted by winter stories of the ancient monks in the red pine, the Benedictine ghosts of Fleury sur Gichiziibi.

Shammer was later named chairman of native studies and straight away he converted the faculty office hideouts to necessary courses of native studies, such as the program to train mongrels to detect the absence of irony, postindian holograms, denivance press, a casino in the library, and the Panic Hole Chancery.

Native students unearthed survivance with wild shouts into panic holes, and easily overcame the crude sentiments of victimry. That obscure chancery of panic revived the old teases of creation stories. The dicey shamans were shouted out at the chancery, and at last the old hoaxers of native medicine were driven to the rich saloons with the lonesome pretenders of the commonweal. The enterprise shamans continued to rattle for the sacred, sleight the spirits, and every time the hokey dance moves were for the money.

Sun Bear, Night Bear, Big Bear, Crazy Bear, Wise Bear, Medicine Bear, name the poseur bears that became sweat lodge shamans to the rich, bored, tedious, and wannabe famous. The overnight bears moved with the easy money, and the motion was never natural.

Panic Radio was the first to report the surprise attack that morning on treaty reservations, and interviewed native citizens who were casualties of the crusade that terminated the democratic government, native continental liberty, and the sovereignty of the White Foxy Casino.

Mason Barrier, the utmost native reactionary patriot, shouted that the end of the tribal police and casino lackeys would turn natives back to real traditions, back to the raw, back to the swish of wild rice, and manly camouflage hunts of survival. Barrier was a chauvinist raised on moose meat, not totems, and with no trace of irony or tease of nature, a character in the old enticement stories of the ice woman. Yes, he could easily have been seduced to rest overnight, forever in the drifted snow. His stories were blunt, punitive, and terminal, the perfect patsy of authority.

Barrier jumped at the chance to announce that he had been arrested several times for the abuse of library books, and was assured that the new sector governor would remove his criminal record and any nasty books shelved in the library.

Harlan Douleur, a retired military radiation technician with bone cancer, waved his tattooed arms and shouted into the autumn night, a blood quantum dream song, for almost an hour on Panic Radio. His voice was pitched with fury about the end of democratic governance, and rage about the return of bloodline politics. He was not a delegate to the constitution but he participated in the four conventions and celebrated the end of the bloody fractions of native identity.

The tone of his voice suddenly turned softer, and then he revealed that his native blood was very thin, as thin as a spider web, an intricate web of true ancestry. Naturally he was very active in the wolf spider totemic council and had advised the government.

Douleur resumed his shouts on Panic Radio that the full blood poseurs had thick blood and heavy hearts, too many hard bumps and thumps to move that brawny blood with an ordinary rush of compassion. Full heavy blood turns blue, and the blue blood fakers in the movies die young.

Rosemary Ogichidaa, a chesty bully who taught native traditions, shifty scopes of epistemology, and indigenous politics at William Warren Community College on the White Earth Reservation, double shouted her phrases, as if to a translator on Panic Radio.

Doctor Ogichidaa, and she insisted on the honorific, was a head-strong nationalist, and a pretender of concocted traditions that were mostly derived from the airs, wares, and obsessions of selective elders. She huffed and puffed in the classroom, and bullied the students with radical talking points that were delivered daily by digital political tags. She conspired with the tradition fascists to block the ratification of the constitution, and she refused to support the citizen referendum, because of modernist connotations of native literature, irony, totemic associations, art, and continental liberty. "Natives were never ironic, never," she shouted on radio, "and irony was never our tradition."

Ogichidaa was dismissive of the totemic councils that advised the autonomous government, and considered bats and spiders a desecration of the original totems in native creation stories. She never associated with mongrels, or any animals or birds, and laughed away the stories that a dog could be trained to detect the absence of irony, because "irony was not native." She was raised with vicious guard dogs, mongrels dumbed down by nasty humans, mostly her father and uncles. The irony mongrels were ready to bark, but were more cautious around the tradition fascist.

Clément Beaulieu, principal writer of the constitution, resisted hearsay as a source of native traditions, rights, and duties. He described the obscure practice of forecast history, the timeworn envies and ideological reduction of stories by selective native elders, as nothing more than gossip theory. His notion of gossip theory was more fully described in his essays on literature, particularly the confidence in culture and highfalutin rumors to interpret creative stories and novels by native authors.

Clément wrote about culture and gossip theory more than twenty years ago, and he repeated the same ideas later on Panic Radio, that no one had to be an expert on classical literature or the Roman Catholic Church to read and teach *Ulysses* by James Joyce, a theologian or anxious altar boy of the Catholic Order of Saint Benedict to grasp the erotic adventures of monks with furry animals in the *Manabosho Curiosa*, or a historian of waves and whales to read the novel *Moby-Dick* by Herman Melville.

Moby Dick has repeated the critical ideas of gossip theory, white pine rumors, and imagination many times when he told stories about the origin of his nickname, the aquarium explorers, and his adventure of the great white whale as a boy in public school.

Clément declared that culture was more gossip than practice, more wild rice hearsay than the play of creation stories and waves of native histories. Native literature was never a doctrine of culture.

Ogichidaa refused to comment on gossip theory, the onanism of wild monks and furry totems, or any ironic stories. She was an assertive but unsteady academic, a stay-at-home ideologue, only slightly published, and her cudgels were raised against modernism, cosmopolitan literature, "postindian chitchat," and any philosophical ideas that were not derived from the conceit of native hearsay epistemology, as she once shouted with great force on Panic Radio.

Ogichidaa, or warrior, was an assumed name.

I goaded the academic warrior that the very concepts of epistemology were not derived from any native thought or creative stories, and the actual sources of native knowledge were more than cultural models, punk structures, learned simulations, or mere contrasts of spirit, shadow, stories, and the seasons. The best native stories were created in motion, never with dominion liturgy, and were never that easy to separate the ideas, concrete or fancy, from mere opinions, conceptions, or the literary traces of traditions and treasures. Ogichidaa waved her hands to stop the interview on Panic Radio. She flashed a perfect toothy smile, and turned away in silence. The native nationalists assumed their terminal creeds were an absolute immunity to critical thought and creative stories.

Ogichidaa was probably highborn because she was arrogant, anxious, steadfast, and overweight, and with teeth so perfect she must have been adopted by a rich family. She walked away in anger after my last question about the fur trade and the signature of continental liberty in the preamble of the constitution. So, doctor warrior, were you actually a descendant of the great fur trade, an advocate of we the people, a union of continental peace and liberty, or were you the guardian of me the people, the *maninaadendam*, a native with an arrogant attitude?

Archive had parleyed with poseurs, fake shamans, federal agents, and many charlatans but only if they had a sense of irony, but he never recognized Rosemary Ogichidaa as a teacher or even as the enemy of the constitution. He was generous with most people, appreciated teases and a lively argument, contradictions, and a native sense of irony, but he never mentioned the tiresome academic ideologues that had endorsed banishment and celebrated the actual termination of native treaties, democratic governance, and the favor of continental liberty.

Archive would rather walk the earth as an exile in the company of other worthy native exiles, or sail forever on the *Baron of Patronia* with the Constitution of the White Earth Nation in hand, than parley for a minute any compromise with the tradition fascists and terminators of native liberty.

Archive reminded us many times that his great-uncle, the principal writer of the constitution, was a native novelist, and no other ratified and citizen approved democratic constitution, in the history of the world, has been primarily written by a literary artist, not the Constitution of the United States, and not the Constitution of Japan.

Rosemary Ogichidaa never returned to Panic Radio.

Archive was moody and uncertain at times, of course, novelists were always in moody motion, but those moments of silence and his avoidance of the tradition fascists were not always predictable.

Godtwit Moon, for instance, was not a teaser, more fascist than creative, and never demonstrated even the slightest trace of native irony. Archive, however, was convinced that the parolee was a rendition faker, and for that reason alone would likely be insecure and ready to participate in the favor and theater of the constitution. The congressional abrogation of the treaty changed the history of the reservation, and the tradition fascists bellied up to the bar with the new sector regime.

Archive and Moby Dick were mistaken about the curse and manner of Godtwit. He turned autocratic and demonic on the very day he was named the governor of the sector, and nothing since then has been the same. Moby Dick has fretted night and day that he might have saved the great explorers, the totemic fish, if he had not pretended to trust Godtwit.

Archive continues to repeat the stories that Godtwit was murdered by angry casino employees, and for good reasons, and he has not ventured another story. I was not there that fateful night of the Debwe Heart Dance so my views of the murder were esoteric, to be sure, that the governor was poisoned by a jealous lover, a younger man he had abused and then abandoned in *Rendition de Gentillesse* at La Maison de Torture Extraordinaire.

More than seven native generations of dissent, derision, and partisan productions, dramatic native plays of policies and contention, ironic traditions, course of simulations, tease and mockery, and the necessary comic scenes with federal agents and senators, authors and romancers of victimry, came to an end forever with that concise notice of abrogation on October 22, 2034.

My ancestors were once removed to the first national theater of elaborate treaties and farcical separatism, and more than a century later the final scenes of that reservation theater in the white pine were staged as a minimal overnight production. I was banished with other natives at the end of that century-old treaty play, and a few days later the new cockamamie theater of national sector endorsements and casino medical centers commenced with the same audience of natives and close-at-hand hearsay elders.

The exiles inaugurated, at the same time, a new theater of survivance in natural motion, the great theater of native continental liberty, and with original scripts, productions, tome talks, ironic parleys, music, and charitable creation stories broadcast every night over Panic Radio on Lake of the Woods.

The Anishinaabe stories of empire have always been scenes of natural motion, waves and water, continuous stories of the fur trade, and that autumn when the treaty was abrogated the exiles created the necessary stories of a new native nation on a houseboat with a modern charter, the Constitution of the White Earth Nation. The constitution resumes the stories of peace and continental liberty at Fort Saint Charles. The native voices of liberty and steady ironic stories were my watchwords every night on Panic Radio.

That morning of the abrogation an emergency meeting of the elected native legislators was convened to review the new sector trust endorsements and the conversion of the casino. The elected representatives and employees were more concerned about their salaries than the actual standing of the constitution and the future of the autonomous native government. Yet, there was not the slightest tease or scratch of sympathy for the legislators who bemoaned the end of the secret monthly cash payments from the White Foxy Casino.

Good citizens shouted out their fears and worries, and once again we shared the inevitable treaty stories, the ironies and stony nostalgia of federal agents. The once repugnant and arbitrary policies of the Bureau of Indian Affairs and the tedious paper salutes to the spacey Honorable Secretary of the Interior returned overnight with similar arbitrary powers invested in the new sector governor and toadies of the White Earth National Sectors and Trust Endorsements.

Mother Teresa, the mongrel healer, moaned, shivered, smiled, and circled the legislators and employees in the conference room. Then with a wet nose and gentle bumps on the thigh of every citizen at the meeting the mongrel assured everyone that natives would survive and continue the government in exile with the mongrel healers. That thought was broadcast late that night on Panic Radio.

Savage Love trained the mongrels to heal, tease, and detect the absence of irony, and that fretful situation, the end of a great constitution of democratic governance was clearly ironic, but that night the irony was unintended, a paradox, a flouted covenant and treaty, and the five mongrels never barked over the obvious.

The *Baron of Patronia* moved slowly toward the old weathered dock abandoned by the Seven Clans Casino on Lake Street at the mouth of the Warroad River. The new native casino on the other side of the river had already been converted as a sector and endorsement center. No other houseboats were moored at the remote dock, located directly across the river from a peninsula and Kakageesick Bay, named in honor of the native who had lived for more than a hundred years on Lake of the Woods.

Panic Radio was a native wave, a nervy wave in the clouds, the natural motion of passion, shouts, and rage, and the *Baron of Patronia* became the new wave of the exiles of survivance and liberty. The stories on the wave became the unforgettable literature of our time, the end of treaties and feigned sovereignty, and a necessary return to native stories and memories in natural motion.

I moored the houseboat to the deserted dock, secured the new navigation instruments, connected the latest global digital passpoint satellite systems to broadcast, set the lithium electrolyte batteries and solar cone devices, and then painted great waves on the deck and cabin of the houseboat, waves that resembled the *Great Wave off Kanagawa* by Katsushika Hokusai. The blue waves started on the bow and curved over the cabin, the Great Wave of Lake of the Woods.

The exiles arrived at the dock about midnight and boarded the *Baron of Patronia*. The great waves were not obvious that night, but the next morning on the international border the teases and stories started over the painted waves. The five mongrels, Mother Teresa, Sardine, White Favor, Wild Rice, and Mutiny bounced on the deck and turned in circles but never once barked because the waves were ironic art. The stories and teases continued for several days about the Giant Wave of Panic Radio.

Chewy was resolute that she would never stand aside as a knit-and-purl senior exile, so she induced her favorite niece to follow the caravan to the abandoned dock that night on the Warroad River. The mongrels raised their heads, and then rushed down the dock to nose and bump the great soprano, but quickly backed away when a circle of nine chickens flapped their wings.

Chewy arrived with two heavy duffel bags and nine fancy chickens. She danced down the dock in slight turns and circles, and sang to honor the ancient natives who lived on the river, and to the memory of Pierre Gaultier de La Vérendrye, the adventurer and first overseas fur trader who established the post at Fort Saint Charles on Lake of the Woods in 1732.

The chickens danced in the manner of the Corn Dance, steady, related moves down the dock and then provided backup musical support with pleasure chirps, peeps, short warbles, and clucks. Chewy gave the chickens tiny chunky peanut butter cookies as a treat for the ceremonial dance on the dock. The mongrels smiled, waited for a treat, and then turned back to the houseboat.

Chewy and chickens were honored as exiles that cold night on the deserted dock, and sworn to endure the winter in natural motion. No one said a word about the inevitable lake ice. The nine chickens and five mongrels were wary, of course, treaded backwards on the deck, and turned twitchy as the *Baron of Patronia* slowly moved away from the dock and sailed into Lake of the Woods.

I charted our first cruise north to Buffalo Bay and then around Northwest Angle near Oak Island and Flag Island to the border near Bukete Island in Canada. The radiant stars could have been the source of navigation, and very early in the morning the *Baron of Patronia* cruised silently on a secure course of the international border.

That first clear night was magical, an extraordinary silence and sense of peace, the two precision engines were barely audible, mongrels, chickens, and the exiles were in natural motion with the bright waves of Northern Lights. The reflection of the aurora swayed on the water with the easy wake of the houseboat, and streams of rose, blue, and green were set in motion at the stern.

I stopped the engines about an hour before dawn and everyone, mongrels, exiles, chickens, waited on deck for the first traces of sunlight. Hole in the Storm raised his hand and gestured to paint the sky, and once again the mongrels were ready to bark.

Mutiny was a fine dancer and moved closer to a cocky Rhode Island Red, waved her lacy ginger tail, and was driven back with clucks and wild wing beats. White Favor pushed his wet nose into the fancy black tail feathers of an Indian Game and was pecked slowly back to the bow of the houseboat. Mother Teresa was poised to heal and bump a Plymouth Rock, and was gently pecked once on the nose. The mongrels and chickens waited at a distance, a narrow escape distance on the houseboat, and in the morning the creature scent was familiar enough to stand closer to each other on the deck. Sardine moaned, Mutiny sneezed, White Favor whistled, and the chickens crowed, clucked, and warbled to honor the glorious glance of sunrise over Lake of the Woods.

The stories about the post at Fort Saint Charles, our new nation of continental liberty, were broadcast on the international border several times that first week of our exile. Panic Radio notices were necessary to establish our presence as the new citizens of peace at the ancient fur trade post. We were exiles but not prisoners, and we were forever in motion with the union of the Constitution of the White Earth Nation.

Justice Molly Crèche, with her river otter medicine bundle in hand, told historical stories on the third night about the murder of French traders at Massacre Island in Lake of the Woods in 1736, two years after the fur post was built at Fort Saint Charles. Justice Crèche announced that Jean-Baptiste, oldest son of the trader La Vérendrye, Jean-Pierre Aulneau, a Jesuit missionary, and nineteen voyageurs had set out in canoes for Montreal. The son of the trader, the priest, and voyageurs were dead on the first night, three hundred years ago, murdered by enemy natives, a sadistic act of revenge for trading with the Assiniboine, Cree, and Anishinaabe. The priest, fur trade entrepreneurs, and adventurers were beheaded on the island, later named Massacre Island. Jean-Baptiste, the priest, and the bloody heads of the voyageurs were buried under the chapel at Fort Saint Charles.

Panic Radio late that night played without notice or an introduction the continuous sounds, the faint clicks, hisses, slight squeals, pitched whistles, and other chatter of hoary bats, and little brown myotis. The late-night sounds of the bat totem were never explained, and no doubt the sector monitors and many other surveillance agencies interpreted the sounds as encrypted messages between native exiles and the partisans of a revolution.

5
HOLE IN THE STORM

The Treaty Shirts were an easy tease, a native coat of arms with singular conference stains, or the à la carte menus of liberty, and only worn by the gutsy crew of exiles with a sense of peace and birthright autonomy.

Zany, of course, and necessary because the original treaty that concocted the reservation conked out at the very start, a party pact delusion and greedy course to the white pine. Treaty Shirts were never worn as protection from evil, corruption, and clearly not a resistance to the scourge of the tradition fascists.

Godtwit cursed our Treaty Shirts.

You know the story, the shirts mocked the treaty not the spirits, not the ghosts, not the sanctuary costumes, not the holy drawers, and only eight exiles continued to wear the shirts, come what may, as a tribute to continental liberty and the busted constitution. The shirts united the exiles for one last cruise of liberty on Lake of the Woods.

My Treaty Shirt was personal not spiritual, a visual recount of artistic sovereignty and creative motion, in other words, the natural bounce and motion of spider webs, the ecstasy of crows in the autumn birch, cardinals in the white pine, and the dicey throwback of the seasons. My revered totem was the spider, and the vision to create the motion and mend the intricate circular webs.

Treaty Shirts were motion, sovereignty was motion, liberty was motion, and the sector masters wore only the masks of fixity and a fade away democracy. Natives once imagined natural motion in stories and art and the ancient portrayals on rocks and caves, ecstatic turns in the evolution of life. Contemporary native artists carried on that visionary perception of motion in stories and the seasons.

October 22, 2034, was a bad day, *maazhi giizhigad*, the new endorsement sector terminated the constitution and native liberty. The treaties were dead and selected natives were once more removed. The White Foxy Casino, already the bane of native sovereignty was turned into a new cash cow and senior sanctuary.

Archive entrusted the exiles to create the counter stories, the cues and ironic scenes of continental liberty for *Treaty Shirts*, the original book of teases and counts of the abrogation and our experiences as exiles. He carried the banners of native motion, and the exiles have carried on the new names and stories of continental liberty.

Yes, my frayed and scruffy white work shirt was an unintended abstract portrayal of hurried meals, salt pork, red wine, paint daubs, smears, and the rainbow spatter of twenty years at conventions and studio easels. The messy shirt was pictured on an exhibition broadside for one of my showy casino scenes at a college gallery. The graze and daubs of colors were brush traces, and the tricky shrouds of my totemic spider signatures and artistic liberty were once boosted by the ethos of the Constitution of the White Earth Nation.

The treaties were done, but new agents were revived on cue to hand out favors in the endorsement sectors. So, the stories of the national crave for dominance on the old federal reservations continues without the old treaties. The sectors were proclaimed not negotiated, and names were revised to serve the delusions of a new pact. The Treaty Shirts became the stained archives of our constitutional past, and a show of native stories.

Archive mocked the treaties, hearsay theories, sector endorsements, and mostly scorned the tradition fascists, but he honored the Great Peace of Montréal. He wore an upland hunter Treaty Shirt decorated with orange forearm patches and padded shoulders, and recounted peace stories to favor native survivance over victimry. The shirt was decorated with a peace emblem on the bow of a voyageur canoe. The token of peace painted on the back of a hunting shirt was a double irony, of course, because of the fur trade, and he was never a hunter. He had always renounced the stories and sentiments of victimry.

The eight exiles aboard the *Baron of Patronia* restored overnight a sense of natural motion and continental liberty, that unmissable gesture of sovereignty that could never be contained or secured in the expectant words and intentional articles of a constitution. Stories with a tease were necessary to avoid the bark of the irony mongrels.

Hole in the Storm was my native nickname, not a birth or sacred name. The nickname was an ironic hint of that great native warrior Hole in the Day, but the name gap or space in the sky was a native tease of my early cubist and grotesque art, the portrayals of heavy reservation hunters and politicians that caused an incredible storm of fault and censure.

My portrayals created storms, and some natives were convinced my art caused bad weather, but the windstorms and dust devil put downs actually inspired me to create even more grotesque scenes of native huntsmen, the eternal lame ducks over casino poker, and the habitual gamers at slot machines.

My casino portrayals were at the heart of the seasons, the calm was at the center of a cyclone, and the hole in the storm of my nickname was that serene moment of creation, that perfect panic hole in the painterly storm at my easel.

Dogroy Beaulieu, my great-uncle, was my art teacher at the Gallery of Irony Dogs located in the First Church of Christ, Scientist near the Band Box Diner in Minneapolis. He was the first native artist exiled from the reservation in the early days of the new constitution, the very document that clearly prohibited banishment. Nothing was ever the same, but that curse of removal turned out to be a favor. My great-uncle became a famous international painter in exile.

We laughed many times about the nasty politics on the reservation, and the native wild cards of an exiled artist in the city. The corrupt decision of the legislative council was reversed, of course, about a year later because of the protests of the president, but my great-uncle never returned to the reservation, not even to attend funerals.

Dogroy wore a tan gabardine military Treaty Shirt, decorated with beaded moccasin flowers on the epaulets, and blue beaded ravens over the breast pockets. He wore that shirt on those moody nights when he told hangout stories about the dark tooth mercenaries on the reservation, or the Midewin Messengers, that motley circle of connivers and blood count acolytes that menaced natives who told ironic stories, or revealed the humor and teases of native traditions or culture. The dark tooth dopers simulated new songs, carried bogus medicine bundles, and turned native totems into a sector pyramid scheme.

The exiles honored traditional art, music, dream songs, and trickster stories, obscure and clever gazers, but never the creepy shamans and holy fakers, or the hucksters, synthetic dopers, and tradition fascists. The dreary tradition mimics were moved more by borrowed liturgy than by the creative origins of stories.

I never worried much about the crazed enemies of the constitution because they were mostly layabouts, deadbeats who carried out only muzzy thoughts, cultish and righteous rituals. Archive, though, was uneasy and convinced the exiles that deadly fascism was in the air, a scary purge of blood and irony, an absolute menace to native liberty, and an absolute threat to the rights created in the Constitution of the White Earth Nation.

Savage Love cornered the tradition fascists with dead words, not with stories, not even with their own stale stories, but with the tacky objects of a dead culture handed over in a last lecture. She borrowed the notion of last lectures, but not the delicacy of nostalgia, from a story by Clément Beaulieu. He created an ironic scene more than fifty years ago about a lonesome priest who renounced his vows and returned to the reservation to convert the poseurs with last lectures.

Father Browne had ordained a tavern in the red pine named the Last Lecture. The pretense shamans, new moon warriors, fakers, and pretenders to the crowns of tradition delivered the last dead words and dubious confessions to a tavern of heavy drinkers and then departed out the back with a new name and culture. Savage Love was precise and accurate, the tradition poseurs would denounce literature, purge the ironic stories of the last lectures, and then raze the taverns in the mind.

Dogroy staged an extraordinary native Opéra Bouffe once a year in the autumn and invited the painters, singers, musicians, writers, tattooed waiters, storiers, and outcasts who lived near Elliot Park, the oldest community in south Minneapolis. I was shied at the first opera, but a few years later my hesitation was overcome with the melodic teases, stray erotic displays, visceral sways, witty, sultry songs, theatrical imitations of animals, and the wild sensual dance moves of the opera players. My heart, voice, and gestures carried me away with natural motion, a native sense of ecstasy. I was never a camp or canoe singer but that night chanted spontaneous fur trade songs, and moved in my imagination with the ancient voyageurs of the woodland lakes. I wore a red cap, shouted out for more red wine, and then chanted a variation of this boat song.

> *let all those change who may*
> *keep to my own mistress*
> *so soft are her eyes*
> *and so tender are her kisses*
> *good old wine makes me doze*
> *but love keeps me awaking*

The Opéra Bouffe players mocked the names of popes, presidents, prominent artists, doctors, and mighty authors, and carried out a marvelous naked and dressy theatrical production with music, songs, stories, and spontaneous erotic dances.

Emily of Praise, Roses, Dog Ears, Lily Lips, Chance, and her daughter Savage Love, lived at the Gallery of Irony Dogs and participated in the comic operas. Savage Love was lusty and wore floaty bright skirts and skintight shirts, unlike her mother who was plainly dressed in baggy jeans and gray sweatshirts, and bound hair, even when she was invited to formally show the clever perception of irony mongrels at the Smithsonian Institution, Department of Homeland Security, and the United States Department of State in Washington.

Savage Love was a savant with words, she teased but never trusted the masters of words, authors, teachers, and politicians, and never tied words to any sense or presence. She was mostly raised in the homey kennel with the irony mongrels and surely perceived as a child the absence of irony in the recitation of stories and in the gestures of social climbers and politicians. She had read many, many books, more than any native could ever name, and yet the words, books, and libraries were never the sources of the seasons, and she never praised or sentenced words to any literary sanctuaries. Yes, you know what she wrote about words, and the treachery of presence. She writes to an absence, not to an exile.

Chance once tried to train abandoned cats, ordinary black and calico domestic alley cats, to detect the moods of irony, not the absence but the aura of irony, because most cats have the natural poise to torment humans who avoided cats. The cats posed and purred at the very heart of irony, not the notice of an absence, but even a mighty purr would never come close to the obvious mongrel bark over the absence of irony. Cats were the actual irony and tease of the absence.

Native storiers created ironic scenes, carried out and trained listeners to favor the contrary tease of expectations, and the tricky stories were necessary to sidestep the obvious deceit of sincerity, hearsay, and authority. Some mongrels learned to bark over the absence of irony, and cats purred at the very nature of irony and ecstasy.

Chance pushed me to consider ecstasy as the natural outcome of irony, and she convinced me that ecstatic visions changed the nature of the world. Right, you know the escort versions of the ecstasy show, that tricky, ironic native stories created cracks in the seams of presence, reversed the notions of creation, and teased the theories of species, blood, breed, ancestors, genre, and the natural motion of colors, avian songs, and the bold feathers of attraction.

Savage Love mocked theories of natural selection as mere nostalgia, the words were not an outcome, not natural, not a choice, and evolution was a dead word from the start. She imagined that ecstatic visions changed the heart, cured disease, turned gills into lungs, pelvic fins into a foot race, the dance of birds, intricate floats of spider webs, caterpillars into moths and butterflies, magic dust, and the shamanic ecstasies of parthenogenesis. The ordinary means of native reproduction, sex, sperm, and fertilization, were never her origin stories.

Savage Love told me at the Opéra Bouffe that she had been conceived by ecstasy, by wild and extreme visions of inception during masturbation with a man, but not by sex with a man. Naturally, she expected the steady teases that follow the opera stories of an immaculate conception in a kennel of irony dogs. Chance, her mother, only masturbated with men, mostly with my great-uncle, but never had sex with a man since she was abused many years earlier on the reservation. Savage Love, her only daughter, was an ecstatic conception of parthenogenesis, and the birth certificate confirmed that very origin story. Chance, the same name for the mother and father, was recorded on the document based on identical genetic signatures.

The Opéra Bouffe at the Gallery of Irony Dogs laid claim to the first perfect native conception in a kennel of irony mongrels with no trace or burden of original sin, and that child has become an exile of ecstasy and my best friend on the *Baron of Patronia* in Lake of the Woods.

My great-uncle was convinced that the blue ravens on his Treaty Shirt would light the spirit of some native artists as protection against that evil strain of concocted traditions that had cursed the original families and good citizens on the White Earth Reservation.

Maybe, but the nasty natives of fortune reproduced overnight and hovered over the nightly slights, mockery, and gestures of comic scenes, creative art, visions, stories, and snarled with stained front teeth at any gaiety, mirth, or wit. The dark toothers cursed the irony mongrels. Yet, some of my distant relatives, cousins on the other side, showed some native humor, and yet hovered at times with the worst of the tradition fascists.

The Midewin Messengers once hired a pack of city thugs to menace my great-uncle at the Gallery of Irony Dogs in Minneapolis. Naturally the mongrels barked at the gate, and within an hour more than a hundred artists, writers, musicians, dancers, tattoo makers, and soused pretenders gathered outside the gallery and shouted down the city deadbeats and mercenaries. Dogroy posed near the gate in a glance of light and the blue ravens shimmered and danced on his Treaty Shirt.

Dogroy was honored around the world for his abstract portrayals, and his celebrated animal and bird shrouds have been exhibited in Paris, Nice, Marseilles, and many cities in Germany. The bald eagle shroud, as everyone knows, has never been shown in public.

The Gallery of Irony Dogs was my sanctuary for more than a year. I watched my great-uncle day and night paint grotesque scenes of natives and animals, and he mocked the baroque masters. Dogroy created *Body Counts*, a series of grotesque portrayals of gory casualties in the wars against birds and animals. The totemic creatures, bobcats, cranes, bears, and river otters were fractured by gunshots, crushed on highways, and devoured by maggots. The fury of the images in *Body Counts* envisioned the massacre of animals in the ancient continental fur trade.

Dogroy wrote that the "portrayals of abstract bodies decayed in public places, a decomposed black bear at the school playground, huge black flies on the withered body of a skunk at the Veterans Memorial near the stone entrance to the White Foxy Casino, and a broken, decayed sandhill crane belted in the backseat of a police car," and more, more, more. He painted a bloody bobcat in a baby carriage, and a gutted river otter in a dental chair. Those scenes enraged many natives on the reservation, and the tradition fascists renounced the series as degenerate, the work of a decadent artist. The community resistance to the accusations and the actual banishment was only slight on the reservation, out of some fear that many other natives would be removed for merely showing some respect for the native visions painted by my great-uncle.

Breathy Jones, the loyal studio mongrel, was always at the side of my great-uncle near the easel, and she was easily shied by a black cat with a heavy purr. Favor nosed the paintbrushes near the easel several times a day, an original custom of cats, and then stretched out on a black velvet pillow and watched my great-uncle paint.

Breathy smiled, a wide wet beam, and sneezed over the absence of irony, a strange encounter, to say the least, and she sneezed at me several times a day but never barked over the absence of irony in my stories, gestures, and in my early painterly scenes.

Breathy Jones smiled and sneezed at me every day because of my eager manner. Favor purred for great artists, a heavy rumble at times, but not for me. I was determined to become an artist, an abstract painter, and in the image of my great-uncle Dogroy Beaulieu.

I never actually painted in the presence of my great-uncle. No one could, no amateur painter would survive the mighty teases, and his great rush of metaphors over the blues, hues, and waves of colors on the canvas. Dogroy was a visionary painter, and he would never sidestep the hearty teases of artists, mongrels, or tradition poseurs.

Dogroy was meditative and sometimes wistful at his first studio in Beaulieu on the Pale of the White Earth Nation. Moses, his devoted cat at the time, watched over his easel and ruled the irony mongrels in the studio. He always painted with the natural sounds of wind and birds and the moody and atonal sonatas of Elliott Carter.

Once banished his gentle manner became more intense, wild and wooly, troublesome, generous, and truly gallant at the Gallery of Irony Dogs. The grotesque and unruly images he painted as an exile could easily turn the surmise of the seasons inside out.

I visited his first studio at Beaulieu on the shore of the Wild Rice River a few times as a boy, but the music, solemn women, animal shrouds, and totemic grave houses, sidetracked my interest in art. I could not fully grasp the subject or practice of masturbation at the time, and the rage of the tradition fascists that masturbation with women was unnatural, evil, and a shamanic curse, might have been enough at the time to weaken an ordinary erection. My great-uncle practiced mutual masturbation with lonesome and abused women, and that practice became something of an operetta once or twice a week at the Gallery of Irony Dogs.

Mutual masturbation, he shouted to the rooftops, was an act of erotic imagination, a generous giveaway for older and lusty visionary painters. Naturally, most people turned and changed the subject of masturbation, and especially the idea of mutual masturbation with women. Yet, the older women at the constitutional conventions were always at his side and ready to praise his creative art.

Moses was a Maine Coon with great white whiskers and he watched over my great-uncle for seventeen years at his studio in Beaulieu. Moses was hanged and dismembered by the dark toothed monsters on the reservation. My great-uncle told me the murder was primeval, and carried out by natives who feared the spirits and traces of motion on animal shrouds, and, of course, the sound of classical music, and his wild and grotesque casino portrayals.

Dogroy praised the obscure images of totemic birds and animals, a vision of the great spirit of animals in his abstract scenes of bright paint, and then created with the great reach of his brush traces of summer in the spring, and the memory of an icy shimmer of winter in the wispy leaves of autumn. Breathy Jones smiled at the side of my great-uncle, and at the same time sneezed over my presence.

My great-uncle created several signature scenes in his portrayals, the slight traces of a moccasin flower, or the crest of a wave, and he encouraged me to create my own obscure totemic signatures in my art. Since then every one of my paintings has a trace of a circular spider web, my totemic union, or the obscure, ghostly image of Frederick Manfred. The Frisian American and jaunty author of the novel *Scarlet Plume* was obsessed with pure warriors and native women, and the faint miniature outline of his face became an ironic turnaround of the literary romancers in my portrayals. Manfred was much more eccentric, romantic, and obsessed in his stories than the German Karl May.

Gichi Noodin asked me to create a late-night broadcast on Panic Radio. The names of many sentimental authors, none were natives, came to mind that cold night on Lake of the Woods. No, the exiles were not ready to hear a tedious survey of the *Primal Mind* by Jamake Highwater, but scenes from the *Scarlet Plume* by Frederick Manfred were high on the list of unintended literary irony. Judith Raveling had been abducted in the novel, an obvious setup of victimry. Savage Love, Waasese, and Justice Molly Crèche practiced the lines from the novel, and the tone, mood, and mockery of their voices created a glorious showdown that cold and clear night of redskin romance on Panic Radio.

Moby Dick started the ironic broadcast with the chancy comments by Arthur Huseboe. He wrote in the sentimental introduction to the novel that the warrior Scarlet Plume was "one of the last pure Dakota Indians, untainted by white ways and beliefs, but doomed himself just as his people are." Yes, one of the early romantic scenes of native victimry.

Wild Rice barked at the absence of irony.

Savage Love read slowly in a revelatory tone of voice a scene from *Scarlet Plume* by Frederick Manfred, "Presently Judith's eye fell on a dusky young woman sitting just across from her in the gate or the horns of the camp."

Justice Molly Crèche continued the narrative in a bold, deliberate, and judicial tone of voice, "Her name was Squirts Milk and she seemed to me to be nursing two little ones, twins, at her ample bosom at the same time. This in itself was unusual enough, until Judith noticed that one of the nurslings was abnormally hairy...."

White Favor barked at the hairy story.

Waasese continued the narrative in a lively tone of voice that night on Panic Radio, "The hairy one wasn't a baby at all. It was a puppy. The puppy's little eyes were closed in bliss as it sucked at Squirts Milk's soft tan pap."

Savage Love continued to read in a serious tone of voice, "She had always admired Scarlet Plume, had even had a love dream about him. How right she had been about him. Once in the long, long ago he had thrown a dead white swan at her feet to warn her that she must fly to save her neck. And he still wished to save her. Yes. Yes. He was more than just a simple red man. He was a great man. . . ."

Mutiny and Sardine barked in unison.

Justice Molly Crèche was steady and descriptive, "His rich, wide lips were those of a lover, graven upon weathered copper. He was all man. A god among men. He made her think of the old Greek heroes: Achilles and Ajax and Odysseus." Yes, and the younger heroes too, she inserted in the scene, and then continued the narrative. "She found it difficult to think him a deadly enemy, a Cuthead Sioux."

The Panic Radio native roundabout irony chats from the deck of the *Baron of Patronia* were especially lively that night. The mongrels barked over the absence of irony in the scenes from *Scarlet Plume*, and the chickens mocked the bay of the mongrels.

Archive repeated the selected roundabout scenes from the novel and the exiles laughed loudest over the "ample bosom," hairy puppy, and "soft tan pap." Manfred was not clear, pap the tit, or pap the food for babies? Surely the pap for puppies, the exiles declared on Panic Radio, was squirted from ample or generous breasts only to tease Manfred.

"The pure untainted Indian is a wild reach to salvation, a perfect godly simulation," said Savage Love

"Manfred delivered dusky women for romantic readers on the western prairie, even in Warroad, Thief River Falls, and Paris," shouted Waasese.

"The hairy puppy at a perfect dusky pap won the Over the Top Mawkish Achievement Award sponsored by the Ruth Beebe Hill Indian Literature Foundation," declared Gichi Noodin on Panic Radio.

Chewy borrowed three lines from "Odysseus," a poem by W. S. Merwin, and sang that night to celebrate the great ironies of weathered and copper men, women, tricksters, gods, and classical heroes, and, of course, native listeners to Panic Radio.

Chewy calmed the mongrels, shied the chickens, and moved the exiles with her marvelous soprano voice when she sang selected lines of poetry by W. S. Merwin.

> *Perils that he could never sail through,*
> *And which, improbable, remote, and true,*
> *Was the one he kept sailing home to?*

Gichi Noodin sailed the *Baron of Patronia* slowly along the international border on Lake of the Woods. The moon was low over the ancient stone, the distant islands of birch and red pine. The water was even, and the exiles were in the natural motion of continental liberty.

6

WAASESE

The Marquis de Sade was a voyageur in the trickster stories of the new fur trade, the erotic *poète de la fourrure*, poet of the fur, and the outrageous bard of weasel sex and beaver peltry carried out his carnal fantasies in birch bark canoes in the colonial tradition of the fur trade fugitives in New France.

That declarative sentence was the start of my satirical novel, *Fur Trade Fugitives*, and yet the ribald narrative never concluded with a book trade denouement. So, think about the continuation of trickster stories and a union of creatures, natives, voyageurs, and coureurs de bois, the runners in the woodland who came together by canoe in that crude and wicked commerce of peltry.

Five natives set out in a *canot du nord*, a north canoe, as the story goes in *Fur Trade Fugitives*, and teased the strange bowsman, decked out in rich brocade and lace jabot, with a catchy nickname, the Marquis de Sade. Natives sang and shouted stories about the nostalgic and lusty voyageurs, the *hommes du nord*, northern men, or *hivernants*, the winterers, and how natives and coureurs de bois once outplayed the fakery and lusty poses of the aristocrats, and continued the same tradition of stories with the Marquis de Sade on the fur trade route to Grand Portage.

The native hunters forever mocked the high culture wars to the very end of the empire fur trade, and in the manner of grey capotes, red toques, and feathery hats. The natives created wild songs, fiddle music, mocked the keep step dances, and imitated the freaky pleasures of heavy party wigs and powders of the royal empire of New France.

The explorers, adventurers, beaver brokers, and empire governors, courted the native chiefs of peltry and tricky diplomats of the fur trade ways. No surprise that the gawky colonial upstarts, and those moody priests in black robes, shunned the showy, erotic stories of the Marquis de Sade, but these pale men soon favored the ordinary sexual teases on a winter night in the woodland.

Jean Nicollet and Pierre-Esprit Radisson, the early risers and continental envoys at large, and Samuel de Champlain, Robert Cavelier, Sieur de La Salle, Comte de Frontenac, Sieur de La Vérendrye, and many other cocky couriers of the empire had their way with native women, and surely with some men in the woodland. The exiles of native liberty were the unintended outcome of that union with the *poète de la fourrure*, the last chance of fur trade surnames and stories of the erotic peltry empires.

Nicollet and Radisson became names of hotels, and Frontenac a resort, La Salle a private school, Champlain a city and college, and La Vérendrye a museum and wildlife reserve, and many other explorers and voyageurs were our ancestors, a union of sex and fur over three centuries with the secure surnames of New France.

The Marquis de Sade narrative was overburdened with surnames and time totes even with the necessary evasions and embellishment of a trickster story. Maybe the best start of a literary legacy would have been a direct pronouncement that the Marquis de Sade had daily freaky sex with ancient mothers, brothers, sisters, the entire totemic associations, and other native fur trade ancestors at the same time in the bow of a great canoe.

Savage Love declared that novels were dead, no matter how they started, wove time, teased, or created evasive and ironic scenes. The words and surnames were terminated in the mighty print of empires, and in the peltry at the back of canoes. Savage conveyed more than once that natives had been declared dead many times in the colonial, military, and cultural histories of the continent, and even more in the coup de grâce of conquest hearsay theories. So, the theme of my novel was extinct, a dead letter tease, because the conquest cultures and fur trade empires were never a presence, and natives were an eternal absence in history.

Clément Beaulieu, the native author who wrote the Constitution of the White Earth Nation, encouraged me to become a writer, a novelist. He praised my imagination, sense of irony, and style, and he was very persuasive, but his generosity was better suited to a much earlier generation of native creative writers.

I mean the traces of literary metaphors and visual scenes were never the same with computers. Too many social network sites courted the ordinary, the constant and tedious personas, and turn of new monitor faces overnight, on the run in an instant, that never became a book of pages with precise pronouns, verbs, and analogies, the repeated structures and seams of literature. The quickie words and contractions, and fast draw locutions of social network websites were never memorable, and not a single word of hearsay ever landed on the shelves of libraries.

Natives were storiers with a natural sense of motion, and the dream songs and stories were always underway in every season of the clouds, and even the best creation stories were never the same one episode to the next. The native dream song, *the sky loves to hear me sing*, was an inspiration to create visual stories, the new trickster stories in the sky, and inspired me to sing, *the sky loves to see my holoscenes*, more than the scenes of my novel.

The turn of seasons, the mismatch of humans, animals, and the fur trade, as you know, were not the terminal scripts of the new alphabet tribes, and natives were never reduced only to the abstract scenes in victimry literature, or the cues of vanished tribes in boorish commercial narratives.

Natives were creative storiers, and natives anticipated the turns of postmodern theories, and natives have written and published critical books for more than three centuries. Churches and missions printed the first native books, and some were narratives of godly discovery and conversions, of course, but those stories of monotheistic revivals were never shouted out to the same sky or natural motion of the clouds with the same spirit as native dream songs, trickster stories, or even the wags of ecstatic shamans. Rightly, the first godly native authors resisted the moronic notions of banishment and the politics of vanished races and victimry.

The fatalistic missionaries of the empire and vengeful gods never heard the dream songs in the clouds, never were enriched by totemic associations, the erotic play in trickster stories, or teased in the same way that shamans teased the reveals of the weather, thunderstorms on the horizon, or the lurk of evil spirits in the red pine. The best native stories, trickster and creation, have always been directed to the sky not to the library. The barren face card similes, kings and queens, and the dead word customs were shouted out back into panic holes.

I turned to the clear night sky, and sometimes to the heavy clouds with laser images, but not with the dead words and weary metaphors of literature. The memorable images were visual and visionary, a new native creation. My laser holoscenes were the new trickster stories in the sky, and in the natural motion of the clouds.

My first holoscenes rescued Samuel Champlain, Chief Joseph, and Christopher Columbus over Bad Boy Lake, and Sieur de La Vérendrye over Lake of the Woods, and many other characters, warriors, and generals, with images from the dead narratives of empire histories. The bright hats and high collars, the laser shimmer of bloated faces, grotesque shoulders, and scenes of flaunty bodies were revived in my holoscenes, or dreamy arenas as they were once recounted in native trickster stories.

The visual scenes of coureurs de bois, native chiefs, and explorers were projected in the night sky, and never once stranded again in the politics of fur trade portages, the revisions of empire narratives, puritans on a mound, or the obscure fame of peace medals and duty of postage stamps.

The uncertain patents of civilization, the trademark of empires, docks, way structures, neoprene, radiant cultural gewgaw, and radioactive bath toys forever washed ashore, the remains of mighty typhoons from other continents, but never a memorable poem, ancient haiku, not even a mushy book, only the scenes of commercial debris forever awash in the oceans. Strange fish and primeval barnacles cruised for many years with the kitschy cultural ruins. Natural motion and exotic cruises were once the source of the great trickster stories of creation, and much older than plastics and global turns of the weather.

I reach forever to the sky with native dream songs, and with light stories and laser holoscenes. The magical streams, buoyancy and vitality, were similar to the natural motion and visual displays in the old stories. Most natives resisted the very idea that a laser holoscene was the continuation of natural motion and trickster stories.

The notion of a singular and exclusive creation was never more than an overworked remnant of colonial and biblical liturgy. Native stories of creation were in natural motion, and creations were only realized in the continuous show of stories. Yet, very few natives today would actually favor the roguish and ironic trickster stories of floods, turds, and recreation on the back of a turtle.

The delightful stories that mock creation, and the ironic stories of ancestors and generations, were cultural traditions in natural motion, the waves and gestures of stories, not the hard grammar of a righteous nativity in a book. The natural motion of holoscenes, turds, turtles, shamans, and trickster stones arise as the new creation stories.

Almost Browne, my father, was one of the first natives banished from his home some forty years ago because he projected laser hologram images over the white pine near Mission Lake on the White Earth Reservation. The new constitution had not been proposed, written, or ratified, but surely that would not have changed the political outcome of banishment.

Almost was banished before Dogroy Beaulieu, the visionary painter, and long before the new constitution. Almost, Dogroy, and the seven exiles have carried out the ethos of native survivance and natural motion to a world outside the venal civics of federal reservations and service sectors.

Homey Saint Roubidoux, the appointed native judge at the time, ruled that natives were haunted by the overhead laser images of explorers and presidents. My father created the name holotropes for the feral lasers, the images of night sky dancers, but the judge had no capacity for irony, and no knowledge of new technology. Homey ruled that the laser scenes were dangerous and desecrated the sacred summer nights on the reservation.

The peace medal presidents might have been tolerated once or twice a summer, but not the aerial green shimmer of Christopher Columbus. The explorer was a laser image, of course, but that distinction was lost as the figure turned in a wide circle, teetered in the twilight, and slowly vanished into the dark water and lily pads of Mission Lake. Some elders worried that the feral light of evil, maybe the devil, had gone under water to bewitch the fish, and waited there for innocent swimmers.

I created feral laser holotropes and scenes in honor of my father, and continued his devotion to the creative spirit of natives and trickster stories. Almost endured the verbal abuse and banishment with courage and good humor, and later he actually unnerved hundreds of ordinary rush hour drivers on the interstate with holotropes of great bears and other totemic animals.

The Mission Lake feral lasers scared some elders, and no doubt the shimmer of the cursed explorer was a fright to other natives, but the glint of great bears on a curve of the interstate terrified drivers, and could have caused serious accidents near the Mississippi River in Minneapolis.

Almost was arrested and charged with endangering the lives of drivers. He was detained in the city jail, but since there were no specific state laser laws my father was turned over to United States Federal Marshals Service and detained as a menace on a federal interstate highway, and for good measure he was considered a fugitive from the White Earth Reservation. Right, he was banished, an exile not a fugitive, but the feral laser images of animals prompted a hearing in federal court.

Justice Marion Troubadour presided at the hearing in federal court and ruled in favor of my father and his ancient inherent rights to create or hunt animals at night with lights, guns, spears, or bow and arrows in any season. One witness testified that the laser projections were similar to silhouettes and the hand shadows of animals. Columbus, the ghostly explorer, and bears on the interstates were almost the same as the historical images on highway billboards or tigers and other animals on breakfast cereal boxes.

Justice Troubadour declared that laser scenes were a creative native gesture, a story, a pen, a computer, the light brush of painted images in the wild night sky, and clearly an inherent native right of laser lights protected by the First Amendment of the Constitution of the United States. She dismissed the dubious federal charges against my father. Naturally, he projected her image that night over the river near the federal court house.

Almost Browne was banished from the reservation, and that arbitrary decision of a tribal judge was not considered a violation of any constitutional rights. How would my father know then that we would share some forty years later the same fate of banishment, at a time when there was a ratified constitution that protected native rights of artistic irony and original totemic associations. The new endorsement sector, however, banished me and other natives and, at the same time, the federal government abrogated the Constitution of the White Earth Nation.

Panic Radio honored my father one night as a great native artist of trickster holotropes, and each of the eight exiles told stories about the laser holoscenes over the rivers and Lake of the Woods.

Godtwit Moon could not wait to exile artists, writers, and the delegates to the constitution, so overnight he posted the handwritten notice of banishment at the entrance to the White Foxy Casino. The seven exiles gathered near the aquariums the next day to tease the day-old governor. He was nervous, stared down at the carpet, and his eyelids twitched. The seven exiles tried to out-tic the poseur, but he was unaware of the mockery. Moon was nervous, his hand gestures were jerky, and he avoided direct eye contact with women, mongrels, and the native exiles.

Clément Beaulieu once told a story about R. D. Laing, the Scottish psychiatrist who had visited a graduate seminar at Harvard University. Laing described schizophrenia as a theory, maybe hearsay theory, but not a scientific model of disease. He said schizophrenia was the light of an ordinary person that broke through the closed minds, a contradiction of modern medicine. Yes, and that singular spirited light of irony was a familiar light in trickster stories. Laing hunched down, ducked his eyes, and never made direct eye contact with anyone at the seminar table.

I thought about that seminar scene many times, the absence of eye contact, and once projected the image of the psychiatrist with huge eyes over the White Earth Hospital. No one said a word about the portrayal, but later my father reminded me that natives were warned to evade the gaze of animals, except irony mongrels, of course, because the eyes of shamans and animals were supernatural, and stares might captivate the insecure. Native hunters looked down and away, sang dream songs, and sometimes survived the wild gaze of bears and predatory animals.

Chewy once told me never to stare down wolves, cougars, snakes, or silent men.

Laing probably could not bear the temper and desire of direct eye contact at the seminar. The graduate students were animals, and the sensitive psychiatrist might not have survived the unintended stares that afternoon. Surely he had tolerated the steady gaze of schizophrenic patients but he was alone at the seminar and could not count on the care and rescue by his close medical colleagues at Kingsley Hall in London.

Chewy convinced me that native totemic connections were more like gestures of eye contact than a handshake, and that a mystical gaze with certain animals and birds was a spiritual survivance, but that ended with the slaughter of animals in the fur trade. Now the exiles stare at spiders, bats, and other new totems in a world of contradictions and rocky ideologies.

Justice Molly Crèche named the new totemic stares at bats and birds, bobcats and crickets, cicadas and fireflies, moccasin flowers and wild roses, the native gaze of liberty. My liberty gazes were laser holoscenes projected in the night sky over Lake of the Woods.

The hoary and little brown bats were my new totems, and the association started as a child with my fascination of the Northern Lights. The connection may not seem obvious, at first, but on some clear summer nights the great streams of light danced in the northern sky, curves, waves, spirals, and the bursts of color, blue, brilliant green, red, and violet. That natural light was the source of my inspiration to create laser holoscenes, as my father had done on many summer nights over the northern lakes, and sometimes the shimmer of laser images merged with a greater natural background scene of Northern Lights. I earned my nickname, Waasese, a flash of lightning, on one of those marvelous nights of natural motion and laser stories in the sky.

Moths, mosquitoes, and other insects sometimes circled the source of the laser lights, but always gathered, or maybe a better notice would be that the insects convened around the outdoor lights at our cabin near Bad Medicine Lake. Yes, a nightly summer convention of insects and naturally the bats circled the lights and caught the insects. The magical dives, turns, swoops, and wide circles of silent bats, and the echolocation of insects around the outdoor lights have always enchanted me. That spectacular scene of natural motion became my totemic association with hoary and little brown bats.

I first created poems and stories about the magic of the Northern Lights, the shamanic giants, and elusive hunters in the sky, of course, and later wrote more abstract scenes of lights in the eyes of animals. I could not imagine why some natives were bored with the stories about natural motion, or those who resisted the genius of trickster stories.

Northern Lights were totems to animals, but humans were never totems to any other creatures. Only mongrels were loyal to humans, but not a totemic association, and the irony mongrels might bark at the absence of irony in the entire gaze of lights and totemic associations. I expected at any moment to hear the steady bark of the mongrels about my visionary union with bats.

Mother Teresa stared at the Northern Lights.

Consider Native American Day, Truman Day, Martin Luther King Day, César Chávez Day, Columbus Day, Rosa Parks Day, and the national Bike, Blood Pressure, Catfish, Oatmeal, Grapefruit, Pizza, and Diabetes months, but not one named celebration of the animals sacrificed in the fur trade. No Beaver Day, Marten Month, or Weasel Season has ever been declared or celebrated. Groundhog Day was the only reference to an animal, a forecast festival based on early weather stories of badgers and bears.

Panic Radio broadcast several times a year a petition for national named animal days, at least one animal day a month to honor the beaver, marten, ermine, bear, fox, bobcat, muskrat, otter, rabbit, deer, wolf, and raccoon. There had never been a designated day or month to commemorate the totemic connections with animals, or a day to grieve for the millions of animals slaughtered in the fur trade for nothing more than fashionable beaver hats, fur coats, and taxidermy.

Almost and his magical holotropes over Bad Medicine Lake and the radiant seasons of Northern Lights inspired me to become a laser holoscene artist, but, as you know, my first creative expressions were literary. My imagistic poems and stories were mostly published online, and several stories appeared in *Transmotion* and other digital journals.

Yet, the old cause of printed books continued to be the measure of a serious literary career.

Trace and Tease Stories, a new website consortium of innovative artists, published *Fur Trade Fugitives*, my satirical novel. Some of the descriptive scenes in my online novel were illustrated with laser lights, and that convinced me that native trickster stories and totems must secure a new artistic practice to show the natural motion of literature.

Native American literature had been crudely reduced to literary theories, and the most vacuous were the hearsay theories of comparative literature that presented linear connections to scenes and native customs, and the crackpot nationalist epistemology of unchanged stories and liturgical traditions.

Hearsay theories, or the theories derived from other abstract models and theories, beget a new ironic *naytive* literary theory. Yes, the necessary prefix *nay* to the theories of native literature that obscured a sense of natural motion and ironic stories. Naytive was a denial, a reference to the mushy naysayers of hearsay theories that restricted the interpretation of native literature to mere cultural themes and victimry.

John Searle was a brilliant theorist about language and metaphor, and his ideas taught me to grasp the great play of words, but his original and learned theories came at the end of ironic, imagistic, and figurative literature. The teases of words and metaphors had already been sacrificed to the instant speech and simile favors of like, like, like, and the impassive cut-and-paste social messages delivered by the next generation of creatures on cellular phones. What, like, what did, like, you mean, like, like, saying literature is like dead? Right, like literature was, like, always dead in the literal similes of social media.

Literary metaphors were original gestures, thoughts, and demanded more than mere literal similes, or the pitch of dead duck comparisons, like, you know, like what does it mean? Native literature has never been like other narratives, and the creative scenes were really not comparable to other cultures or models. Right, not comparable previous to the dead similes of the vanishing race and victimry.

The language and words may remain the same but the meaning of the metaphors and the interpretation of ironic literary scenes were seldom comparable because the traces of meaning were original in native thought, and in creation and trickster stories. Native American literature was wounded in the academic wars of hearsay theory and dead letter comparative studies, a casualty of literary combat with the patrons of victimry.

Computers and social media similes have no sense of irony, and no consciousness to perceive natural motion in native literature. The intentions of computers and social media were relative, not creative, and the chances of literary metaphors, textual teases, or traces of irony were at best unintended.

Almost Browne, my father, taught me how to create new laser holoscene images, and retrieve in natural motion the obscure metaphors, irony, and teases in native trickster stories. My laser holoscenes were figural images that were based on traces of a historical presence, however elusive or enhanced, and were original ironic portrayals in the night sky. The artistic abstractions were in the laser projection and motion, not in the fractured beams or shimmers of light. The laser images were always in motion, and slowly dissolved in the manner of trickster stories, but not in the classical literary theory of denouement.

Panic Radio surprised Savage Love with a special late-night program of thoughts and ideas about nature by Sigurd Olson, the philosopher of the wilderness, and especially the natives and voyageurs in the ancient fur trade. Savage Love never raved about many writers, but she adored the gentle mentor of the woodland lakes, Sigurd Olson.

Continental Prosesphere, once named the Tracesphere Library, provided easy access to hundreds of thousands of books in the clouds, so there was no need to carry bound books, but Savage Love packed her own favorite library, and she read only printed books. She always traveled with nine books, *Straw Dogs* by John Gray, *The Stranger* by Albert Camus, *The Unnamable* by Samuel Beckett, *Moby-Dick* by Herman Melville, *The Heirs of Columbus* by Gerald Vizenor, *The Narrow Road to the Deep North* by Bashō, *Claiming Breath* by Diane Glancy, *Survival in Auschwitz* by Primo Levi, and *The Lover* by Marguerite Duras.

Savage Love never carried books by Sigurd Olson and only mentioned the writer to certain friends because, she argued, most people would not understand his ethos of the wilderness. So, when selected sentences from his books were broadcast that night she rushed onto the deck to listen and to watch the rise of my holoscenes over the bow of the *Baron of Patronia*.

Panic Radio programs were broadcast every night to thousands of loyal listeners in Canada and the United States. Surely the listeners could imagine my holoscenes, the laser image of Sigurd Olson. His rugged face was transposed and merged with various animals, a beaver, bear, wolf, moose, and bat, of course, and naturally the mongrels howled and barked at the images in the night sky over Lake of the Woods.

Gichi Noodin slowly read the first two selections from *Reflections from the North Country* by Sigurd Olson, and then Chewy charmed Savage Love by singing the other two selections from the book. Later, at the end of the songs the exiles talked about the ideas, teased the romantic prose of the woodsy author, and delivered the usual wordplay and ironic radio comments on Panic Radio.

> *While I have known many frontiers over the continent, it is the era of the fur trade and exploration in the Northwest that has intrigued me most. I never lost my love of it or the thrill of following those ancient routes and facing the challenges voyageurs met when the Northwest was still unknown.*

The *Baron of Patronia* was cruising on the international border in the same lake that the voyageurs once paddled in great birch bark canoes, and the same woodland lakes that captivated Sigurd Olson. Savage Love watched the images of the author move slowly overhead, a spectacular laser journey with the exiled ancestors of the voyageurs.

> *I watched a couple of canoes beating their way across the open reaches of the lake. The boys in them were singing and I caught snatches of their song. Stripped to the waist, they were using their brawn to keep the slender craft from getting out of line in the gale. Traveling by primitive means, I knew within them the long inheritance of a nomadic ancestry was surging through their minds and bodies, bringing back the joy of movement and travel, adrenalin pouring into their veins, giving courage to muscles being strained to the utmost.*

Chewy raised the microphone, and the nine chickens and five mongrels circled to hear the marvelous sound of her voice, a clear, emotive, and steady soprano timbre under the brilliant stars and my catchy holoscenes. Panic Radio was the last original voice of native continental solidarity and liberty. Savage Love turned toward the bow and reached for the sky as she listened to Chewy sing the romantic stories of Sigurd Olson.

Men who had never sung a note before
bellowed songs into the teeth of the wind,
faces that at the start showed grimness and strain
soon began to relax.
I have noticed when traveling with Indians
that they often break into song when on the move.

Morose and unhappy in camp
and often irritable with the drudgery
and work of preparation,
once they were on the trail things changed
and they sang and, after supper was over,
make music as only Indians can.

Moby Dick initiated the late night ironic banter and tricky wordplay on Panic Radio. The session started with a tease, of course, and the exiles shouted out words of love and devotion, *beloved wordy, dearest scribe, charity word boy of the wilderness, ardor in a canoe,* and *lust on the portages,* to mimic the author Sigurd Olson.

Savage Love returned from the bow of the houseboat and waved her hands to protest the tease of the author, but when the mongrels bounced and barked, and the chickens clucked and crowed, she was coaxed enough to laugh and join the mockery of the sentimental prose about the ancient voyageurs.

"Sigurd Olson declares his love and thrill of the fur trade, but never mentions the slaughter of animals, native diseases, the hardship of the voyageurs, the desertion of totemic names and associations, or the deceit of the Beaver Club in Montréal," shouted Justice Molly Crèche on Panic Radio.

Clearly the mood of the mockery changed to a serious critique, and rightly so, because the gentle and nostalgic narratives of the fur trade and deadly frontier served only the sentiments of a mea culpa culture and victimry. That very same nostalgia of the vanished race, and the strained romantic narratives of cultural histories have been the most popular themes published in literary essays and books about natives.

Hole in the Storm mocked the fantasy of brawny boys in a slender canoe, and, of course, the primitive means of travel was an inheritance of nomadic ancestry. So, Sigurd Olson, whose nomadic ancestry do you have in mind, native or French? Totemic or colonial fur traders? The notice of brawny boys invited a more discreet hermeneutics of sexual fantasies and the fur trade voyageurs, and anticipated the stories in my novel, *Fur Trade Fugitives*, about the voyageurs and the Marquis de Sade.

Savage Love stared in silence at the microphone, and then sheepishly smiled and revealed, "Sigurd Olson, that lanky, wrinkled, moody man of the wilderness was an easy reminder of my literary love of Samuel Beckett, the novelist and poet. Beckett was lanky, wrinkled, a moody man of Paris. Sigurd Olson was my wrinkled man of the Superior National Forest."

Mother Teresa bumped Savage Love on the thigh with her wet nose, Wild Rice licked her hand, and three chickens stretched their wing and sickle feathers. The revelation, or confession, about lanky lovers set a more serious tone, but only for a moment. Sigurd shivered, threw a kiss, and then my laser image of the author vanished in dark water.

Gichi Noodin leaned closer to the microphone and in a sporty tone of voice announced that the wrinkled authors Sigurd Olson and Samuel Beckett were the miraculous double reincarnations of Jean Baptiste La Vérendrye, the young decapitated voyageur buried at Fort Saint Charles. White Favor whistled on deck, and the other mongrels moaned and feigned a bark. The nine chickens swayed in silence on the rails of the houseboat.

Savage Love, late that night at the end of the teases and mockery, restored her morose manner with heavy last words on Panic Radio. She selected two short sentences from the *Unnamable* by Samuel Beckett, and read slowly with a deep and moody tone of voice. "Strange task, which consists in speaking of oneself. Strange hope, turned toward silence and peace. Possessed of nothing but my voice, the voice, it may seem natural, once the idea of obligation has been swallowed, that I should interpret it as an obligation to say something. But is it possible?

"I don't know, I'll never know, in the silence you don't know, you must go on, I'll go on." Savage Love closed the program that night with these words, "Silence, I must go on, and going on with the exiles, irony mongrels, and memories of Sigurd Olsen and Samuel Beckett."

7

JUSTICE MOLLY CRÈCHE

Native totemic unions were ancestral and character related, and the unions were continued for personal reasons in the stories of treaty fugitives. The exiles honored totemic connections, celebrated the scenes, stories, and birthright of continental liberty, and forever renounced that crude rein of endorsements and sector servitude.

The cause of creature justice, animals, birds, and other spirits of creation, the usual turns of stories, easily evolved in contemporary native literature, but scarcely a trace of animal rights appear in the histories of predatory empires, monotheistic cults, or chemical cultures.

Totemic justice originated in native stories and in the consistent evidence of creature connections, navigation, and intuitive care. You know, the recognition of a spirited way of life, tease of flight, hibernation, pollination, echolocation, and the entirety of natural motion, created the egalitarian principles of totemic unions, or connections that were more intimate and consequential than the mundane reciprocity of material cultures.

The weighty chronicles of enlightenment were easily discounted in native stories as unintended irony, and the steady mongrel barks were surely heard at the start and much later at the abrogation of reservation treaties, and, of course, the barks at the end of so many wars.

Monotheism and the late-night promises of civilization were seldom the most reliable sources of equitable evidence, totemic justice, or native continental liberty. Yet, so many natives were converted to that easy notion of a single fearsome creator, with angels and demons on the sly, to oversee the pious mission of the cruel separation of animals from humans.

The Constitution of the White Earth Nation created a momentous aura of native survivance, an overused concept in critical literature, of course, but the notion of new totemic connections and resistance to cultural corruption became a source of personal motivation, of praise, insight, irony, and the ethos of restitution over retribution in my decisions of the tribal court.

Archive described the creation of the constitution as a narrative of moral imagination. The notions of a creative spirit and communal duties were common in native stories, and Edmund Burke introduced the concept of a moral union more than two centuries ago in *Reflections on the Revolution in France*. Native creation stories were always a tease of moral unions with humans and animals, and trickster stories were more perceptive of natural motion, the turn of seasons, and more persuasive than the violence of revolutions.

I was the first elected senior judge of the constitutional tribal court, and at the time even the old enemies of the new constitutional governance and autonomous judiciary had advocated my election to the new court. The respect for my philosophy of cultural restitution, however, soon turned to nasty hearsay when the court carried out regular hearings on the natural rights of birds and animals, and the recognition of legal standing for totemic creatures in court.

The animal rights sessions were always scheduled at the end of the day and never detracted from the necessary duties of the court, such as domestic abuse, child protection, foreclosures, fraud, forgery, and mostly violations of the Variable Chemical Synthesis and Controlled Substances Act. That consideration, however, never reroutes the constant harangues of the tradition fascists over the equal rights of sleeve creatures, Bichon Frisé and Chihuahua, the designer choices of casino gamers and black tooth narcotics crazies.

Most native citizens were eager to participate in the new government, and in the first year seven new totemic community councils were established, mostly based on the traditional totems, loon, bear, marten, and sandhill crane. These more common totems were easily resumed with the conscience and moral union of native ancestry. Regrettably many natives fiercely opposed the new bat, coywolf, and wolf spider associations as perversions of the ancient practices. Yet, several months later the legislative council voted to approve the three new totems. The Bichon Frisé, however, was never considered as a native totem.

The other more reasonable critics of my decision to protect creatures would consider restitution for some totems, but not outright equal rights for spiders, bats, or coywolves because most natives would not associate with the totemic names of pests and predators. The reminder that bears and eagles were predators was not persuasive.

No one could ever forget that during the constitutional conventions the tradition fascists had denounced everything mixed, mingled, or crossed, totemic animals or humans, and refused to acknowledge coywolves for the same reasons they renounced the natural rights of native crossbloods as citizens of the White Earth Nation.

I scheduled late-night sessions in tribal court to hear testimony about the abuse of spiders, wolves, bats, and other creatures, and to establish the legal standing of the coywolf, hoary bat, and wolf spider as new totemic associations duly recognized by the legislative council. The children at the session were very excited to hear stories about spiders, but some of the elders, mostly women, cringed over the mere thought of a spider totem council, and suggested that webs would be a wiser political totem.

Harlan Douleur had initiated the wolf spider totem to the legislative council and then testified that his native blood ran very thin because of medication and his ancestry. He praised the constitution and the practice of the court that honored the heart and conscience of native totems, and related how he sat on the screen porch and watched spiders build and repair webs during his long recovery from cancer. "Spider webs are intricate and shimmer in the morning, a beautiful scene as thin as my blood, a web of native spirit and fur trade ancestry," he testified. Douleur was a retired army sergeant with bone cancer. He raised his right arm to salute the court and revealed an elaborate tattoo of spider webs on his forearm.

Hole in the Storm created a union with the spider as his personal totem, and as one of his painterly signatures, but he did not actually specify the wolf spider.

The tradition fascists arrived late and dominated the court testimony with an intense censure of the wolf spider and coywolf totems as obscene notions of the original and true native totemic traditions.

Butchy Manson shouted, "The wolf is a sacred totem, and not a coyote, never a coyote or coy mixedblood, and the coywolf does not belong in our traditional totems or songs on the reservation."

Naturally, she had not considered the contradiction of precise native traditions secured on a federal reservation. Butchy refused to consider that natives had been removed more than a century earlier from diverse native communities at the miserable end of the slaughter of sacred native totems in the continental fur trade.

"Our ancestors never heard of coywolves, so how could that coy thing be a totem?" said an older woman who lived in the senior residence.

"French coywolves," said Moby Dick.

"Wolves are sacred, and never were spiders, so we condemn the use of the sacred totem of wolves to name a creepy imposter, and only a birdbrain would think spiders were wolves," said Micky Crow.

The court testimony on the rights of creatures was never conclusive, as everyone knows, yet the number of enthusiastic spectators increased as the sessions continued one night a week as totemic entertainment for more than a year. Surely the most persuasive testimony was about the outright murder of animals in the fur trade, and the murder of birds in the freaky fashion trade of decorative feathers. The testimony on several nights turned to the despicable plume hunters who murdered snowy egrets, golden eagles, bald eagles, cardinals, and hundreds of other birds.

The Migratory Bird Act of 1918 provided protection for some birds with decorative feathers to live at peace in the same world as humans. The cruelty of that predatory war against animals and birds was countered and never excused in the worthy notice of new totemic connection with many other creatures, birds, bats, flowers, and spiders.

The rise of deadly diseases caused by lethal pathogens that moved from animals to humans scared many people to turn away from animals, totemic associations, and continue the crude sacrifice of other creatures for the race of material culture. Fox, raccoons, deer, and many other animals moved to the cities to avoid human predators and deadly poisons of agriculture.

Everyone who appeared in tribal court has heard me talk about the philosopher John Gray, and ideas from his books, *Straw Dogs* and *The Silence of Animals*. Sylvia Beach, the librarian, told me there was never a rush to read more about his critical thought because the books were published more than twenty years ago. Not surprising, the number of books acquired by the library more than doubled in the past decade, and at the same time there was a comparable decline in the actual number of books that were borrowed at the library. Natives prowled the global networks with other creatures of the night, but seldom visited a library. Today hardly anyone reads more than a few pages of electronic captions in a day.

Continental liberty was a caption.

Totemic unions were captions.

Animals were captions.

The seven exiles were captions.

Those who testified in court on totemic animal rights heard me repeat several times a selection from *The Silence of Animals*. "The distance between human and animal silence is a consequence of the use of language. It is not that other creatures lack language." Yes, of course, and much more, consider the silence of gestures and the animal gaze. "The discourse of the birds is more than a human metaphor. Cats and dogs stir in their sleep, and talk to themselves as they go about their business."

Gray had obviously not come in contact with the irony mongrels, or he might have mentioned the sustained barks over the weary digests of philosophers. "Humans are the void looking at itself. It is a lonely image. But why privilege humans in this way? The eyes of other creatures may be brighter. Humans cannot help seeing the world through the veil of language."

White Favor and the other irony mongrels were trained to bark at that curtain of words, the uncreative mishmash of tense, cause, person, dopey similes, and the obvious absence of irony. Totemic unions were visionary, creative stories that reached over the captions, hand mirrors, and cultural cants of the moment.

Gray declared that myths, and clearly he should have more clearly discerned native myths from hearsay theories, were "inherited from religion," and the humanists were "ruled by myths, though the ones by which they are possessed have none of the beauty or the wisdom of those they scorn." Gray created original ideas about animals, but he could have been wiser with a visit to my court sessions on animal rights. Surely not many heavy-going humanists could bear the actual gaze of an animal, or the totemic stories of other creatures.

The gaze of animals continued in stray trickster stories, and the gaze of bears, wolves, or lynx was seldom averted with the disguise of hunters. The doctrines of the other, the gawky hunter in camouflage, the ruse of sounds, scents, and blinds, never lasted as a tricky evasion or escape from the gaze of animals. The gaze of the other was always there, or, to turn that gaze around, humans remained forever in the eyes of the other, in the magical eyes of bobcats, the steady stare of coywolves, and always in the compound eyes of blowflies. The gaze was bright and nightly, even in a trance, or a nightmare.

The court names and calendars of evolution created the disguise of the other, the animal other in monotheism, and natives were once wrongly considered the other creatures in the course of enlightenment and hus- bandry. The corrupted animals of civilization wore weighty clothes, giant wigs, top hats, spats, whalebone hoopskirts, and heavy powders to escape the gaze of the natural world. Some men coveted the picture postcards of naked native women, and revealed the perverse traces of the naked other. Many natives mocked the poses and evasions of the animal gaze with top hats, epaulets, and morning coats.

The gaze continues to uncover cultural disguises, and at the same time natives created a vital presence of the natural gaze in totemic unions, and without the evangelical shame of nudity. There were many other native gazes, the shamanic gaze, the ironic gaze, wild adventures gaze, and stories that disguise the liberty gaze, glory gaze, erotic gaze, hunter gaze, godly gaze, hunger gaze, pity me gaze, and the gaze of victimry. Na- tives were once captured in the literary and predatory gaze of victimry.

My nickname, clearly derogatory and ironic, was first delivered in court in the third year of my term as an elected judge. I had mounted a miniature totemic crèche of animals and birds, bears, beaver, coywolves, bats, sandhill cranes, and bobcats decorated with spider webs during the winter solstice at the entrance to the tribal court. The crèche was clearly a source of pleasure for most natives, a gesture of totemic irony, but the tradition fascists destroyed the original totemic images as a desecration of the sacred totems of natives. The totemic animals, papier-mâché and painted clay, were actually created by schoolchildren. This was one of those rare events when the fascists and the various solemn monotheists and evangelists connected overnight to censure my totemic creature crèche. Since then the crèche nickname has become an obvious source of necessary irony in the secular deliberations of the tribal court.

Totemic associations, animals, birds, and spiders, have always been represented with an evocative presence or legal standing in my court. The standing of a vital spirit and dear life was broadly accepted in my courtroom because of the undeniable evidence that animals, birds, trees, and insects were abused, poisoned, and terminated by humans, institutions, and corporations.

The white pine and other trees on the White Earth Reservation, for instance, had been removed from treaty land by sweetheart agreements between timber companies and agents of the federal government. The forests were ruined by clear cuts, and the consequences were adverse to natives and other creatures of the environment. The white pine treaty forests had rights and legal standing in my tribal court, and the historical testimony established the willful destruction of natural stands of ancient trees.

The animals, beaver, bear, marten, and ermine, hunted and murdered in the continental fur trade, were recognized with legal standing in tribal court. The court testimony by native storiers and some historians provided the ostensible evidence necessary to pursue selected indictments of the coureurs de bois, prominent voyageurs, four colonial empires, constitutional governments, resource enterprises, chemical corporations, and the institutions, museums, and individuals who collected, displayed, and benefited from the legacy and serial murder of animals in the fur trade. The exiles grieved for the spirits of forsaken creatures.

The possession of stolen native property, sacred objects, and animal body parts, skin, skull, bones, paws, claws, and bear teeth, must be considered criminal evidence of the fur trade massacre. The purchase of totemic animal pelts and stolen remains was a crime. Taxidermy and embalmed animals and birds would be considered criminal in totemic justice, no less a criminal practice than the hideous display of embalmed and positioned human skeletons in museums.

My totemic medicine pouch, a personal and revealed connection with the spirit of the river otter, caused many natives to rush me in tribal court with harsh derisions and accusations of hypocrisy. The tradition fascists cursed me, that my sacred pouch, or medicine pelt, was a desecration of totemic traditions. The accusations were based only on the presence of peltry, and with no recognition of the actual evidence and native stories that honor my totemic union with the river otter.

Peter Vezina, a native healer, shamanic visionary, and maybe a member of the *midewiwin*, the medicine dance, had created the medicine pouch some two centuries earlier at the time of the fur trade. The abandoned pelt was recovered from the ice on the shoreline of Muskeg Bay in Lake of the Woods. The otter pouch contained sacred stones, *miigis*, or the revered shells of native motion, curative herbs, flowers, found wing bones and feathers to heal stray native spirits, the heavy beat of hearts, and to restore memories and the visionary presence of native ancestors.

An army medical doctor plundered that very sacred pouch from the cabin of a native healer in the Battle of Sugar Point near Bear Island on the Leech Lake Reservation in Minnesota. Natives that morning had outmaneuvered and soundly defeated the Third United States Infantry in 1898 by ingenuity, spirited stealth, and by courage, but the soldiers looted a sacred pouch, a war necklace, and other ceremonial objects as war booty.

Peter Vezina reported the military plunder of sacred objects but the army, and federal agents on the reservation, disregarded the cabin burglary and any blame for the theft of the medicine pouch by an army officer.

Pierre Vezina, grandson of the native healer, and my father, was told a century later that a "Bear Island War Indian Medicine Bundle" was posted for sale at auction in Paris, France. Pierre, two senators, and other members of my family petitioned that the auction house return the stolen pouch, but the director would only account for the current owner, a historian and reputable collector of native art. The auction house declined to intervene with any accusation that the pouch was stolen, even though the provenance revealed that the pouch was once owned by an army medical doctor who served in that capricious war against natives at Sugar Point near Bear Island.

Pierre raised several thousand dollars from the family to secure the otter pouch at auction in Paris. My father had never traveled outside of the country, but he had repeated many of the stories told by our relatives who served in the American Expeditionary Forces in the First World War and in the Second World War in France. So, he was readied by native visionary stories to encounter the actuality of our fur trade ancestors in France.

Pierre was at the auction house early to examine the medicine pouch. The security agents were concerned that my father might disrupt a commercial auction with a scene of totemic repatriation. Rightly, he considered a dramatic rescue of the sacred family medicine pouch. Yes, arrested with the pouch in hand, the newspapers might report, and my father was convinced the general public would have been sympathetic.

My father was left behind at the start of the bidding, and could only watch as the price reached a much higher amount than the family provided to buy the pouch. The sole bidder and final purchase was more than twice the reserve price at auction. My father was downhearted, of course, but as he was about to leave the auction house a security agent directed him to a private room and, as he told the story for many, many years, the spirit of the river otter was present at the auction and inspired an extraordinary scene of native and totemic liberty. The pouch was covered on a shiny display cabinet, and my father was about to show his rage when a lovely woman entered the room, extended her hand, smiled, and then uncovered the sacred medicine pouch.

Penina Crémieux, the historian and private collector of native art, was the final bidder at the auction. She raised the final price only to secure and return the pouch to my father and the family. My father was in tears, of course, and later that year she participated in a creative river otter ceremony on the White Earth Reservation.

Penina was the granddaughter of Nathan Crémieux, who once owned an art gallery, and she heard stories about Aloysius Beaulieu, the native artist who painted blue ravens and served with his brother, Basile, in the First World War in France. Nathan had featured the distinctive blue ravens at the Galerie Crémieux on Rue de la Bûcherie near the Notre Dame Cathedral in Paris. Aloysius the painter, and Basile Beaulieu, the writer, moved to Paris after the war and never returned to the White Earth Reservation.

Nathan Crémieux sold almost every portrayal of blue ravens, abstract scenes of war, bridges, and the city, painted by Aloysius. They were very close friends and worked together on the presentation and exhibition of contemporary native art in Paris.

Penina told stories about one of her ancestors, a double great-grandfather, a pioneer in the early eighteen hundreds who traded dry goods, jewelry, and sundries for native pottery, art, blankets, and other objects in the American Southwest. That original collection of native art, but never sacred objects, was inherited by her grandfather Nathan and became the signature collection of the Galerie Crémieux.

Then, in 1943, the French police removed Nathan with thousands of other Jews to the deadly Drancy Internment Camp, and the Nazis seized the entire gallery of native art, blue ravens, pottery, trade blankets, sashes, ledger art, and other native objects. No doubt some of the plundered native art and blue ravens were later mounted in the homes of chosen Germans.

The White Earth judiciary ordered the repatriation of native art, notably the plundered series of blue ravens by Aloysius Beaulieu, and the court was prepared to prosecute as war criminals those citizens who had received native art and property stolen from the Galerie Crémieux. The court avoided state and national agencies and proceeded directly with the prosecution of the criminals a few months before the abrogation of the treaty reservation, and the demise of the native constitution and judiciary.

Godtwit Moon, the sector governor, had been ordered by federal agents to undermine the authority of the tribal court and egalitarian government. That, as most natives know, was not the end, never the end, but rather the start of native stories, original stories of exile, survivance, and continental liberty on Lake of the Woods.

Old John Squirrel was not a familiar name in the course of legal education or native justice but his name has always been a presence in my tribal court as a reference to the new sources of evidence in stories. Yes, a creative presence of native evidence. Native stories have been slighted as mere hearsay in state and federal courts, as everyone knows, but that has never been the rule in the judicial tradition of the White Earth Nation.

Charles Aubid, an inspired native storier and a witness in federal court more than sixty years ago, mentioned the name Old John Squirrel in sworn testimony. Aubid was in his late eighties at the time, and recounted visual scenes from the late eighteen hundreds in concise, substantive, and visual stories as court evidence, and with an obvious sense of natural reason. The stories created the presence of Old John Squirrel in court, a sense that he was a fourth person, a visual presence in various perspectives, more than a second or third person in stories.

Aubid and other native witnesses were in federal court to convince the judge to restrain the government agents from regulating the wild rice harvest. Clearly natives understood the traditional harvest and had the inherent right to regulate and gather *manoomin* or wild rice on treaty land and wildlife refuges.

Aubid testified though translators that he was present as a young man with Old John Squirrel when federal agents declared that natives always had the right to decide the actual time to harvest wild rice in the autumn. The federal prosecutor objected to the stories about Old John Squirrel as hearsay. The judge pointed out that the court recognized only direct knowledge from the witness. Aubid smiled and then continued the same story but from another visual perspective. The prosecutor raised the same objection to hearsay.

United States District Judge Miles Lord told Aubid that Old John Squirrel was dead, and "you can't say what a dead man said." Aubid leaned closer to the judge, pointed at the stack of legal books on a table, and shouted that the books contained only the stories of dead white men. "Why should I believe what a white man says, when you don't believe John Squirrel?"

That report about hearsay, evidence, and precedent was published in the *Minneapolis Tribune* on September 13, 1968. Gerald Vizenor, a native journalist at the time, wrote the story and clearly anticipated the later decision of the International Criminal Court that "relevant and necessary" hearsay was admissible in testimony.

The Old John Squirrel stories were considered relevant, inspired, and clearly necessary, and Justice Miles Lord ruled in favor of the native right to regulate the wild rice harvest. Native stories were considered credible evidence in tribal court, and yet native stories were never the same from one scene to another in visual memory, so several stories were necessary to create a greater perspective and sense of the evidence, the presence of a fourth person in native stories.

The fourth person in native stories was a creative presence of a character, not a historical presence, and not hearsay theory, but a persuasive image in a scene created from a visual memory of a situation.

These court stories became an original literature of native reason and legal procedures, but the practice ended with the abrogation of the reservation treaty. The stories of native precedence and evidence continued in exile, and in a new native venue named Panic Radio.

My father posted that news article on the sideboard with tribal council notices and family photographs. I was ten years old at the time, and we lived in a cabin near Spirit Lake on the White Earth Reservation. Old John Squirrel, Charles Aubid, and Justice Miles Lord were in our cabin and memories, but my meander to law school was more chance and totemic than the inspired stories of legal precedent.

Chewy and the seven exiles were the new storiers, and our personal recounts in *Treaty Shirts* created an archive on the other side of the court and constitution. Naturally the stories became literary precedence, original accounts of continental liberty at the end of the reservation treaty, and the finale of century old counter stories of degenerative governance that gave rise to the Constitution of the White Earth Nation.

Natives have always told stories about situations of separation, exclusion, and exile from other cultures and states, from the fringe of colonial cults, the missionaries of deadly diseases, reservations and salt pork, commodity cheese and booze, law schools and exile, and yet natives in the gaze of demons have outwitted the federal managers with an egalitarian constitution. That constitution, totemic associations, and an ethos of native egalitarian governance, were diminished, as everyone now knows, by the sleeper agents of congressional plenary power, and in the same brute transaction of dominance, the constitution was contravened by federal endorsement sectors. The seven exiles started new stories and created ironic and tricky scenes of the fugitive constitution in natural motion. The stories of exile were broadcast every night on Panic Radio.

Samuel Beckett was overhead that cold night, and his laser gaze aroused the chickens, mongrels, and shivered over the bow as the exiles read creative selections of lines from *Waiting for Godot* on Panic Radio.

The Baron of Patronia cruised on the calm international border of Lake of the Woods and broadcast concise scenes of the famous play. No one clearly understood the existential dialogue, but the exiles never missed an ironic gesture in the play.

Waasese projected the lanky body and wrinkly face of the author, and the laser images of two other characters from literature and the fur trade. She was creative in every sense, the laser gaze and faces in the night sky that would never otherwise meet in the world. The laser images of Beckett, La Bonga, the voyageur, a mighty fur trader and freed slave, and Sylvia Beach the emissary of books, and with a sly smile, gestured to the exiles and mongrels on the *Baron of Patronia*. White Favor ran to the bow and whistled at the laser image of the librarian.

Waasese had actually merged two images into one recognizable face, the bookstore owner from Paris, of course, and the reservation librarian with the same nickname. Sylvia Beach shimmered, separated at times, and then the laser faces united closer to the images of Beckett and La Bonga, the two exiles in the night sky. The chickens clucked in circles. The mongrels nosed the air, and Sardine moaned, sneezed, and bounced on the deck. Beckett was an exile in France, La Bonga was an exile of slavery in the fur trade, and together that night we were exiled natives, laser authors, and book emissaries of continental liberty.

Savage Love was surprised by the tease, and rushed out on deck that night to watch her favorite author shimmer over the cabin, and then circle the *Baron of Patronia* with La Bonga and Sylvia Beach. The holoscenes gestured toward the horizon, and then turned in the other direction.

Savage Love mimed in silence the concise words and pithy gestures of *Waiting for Godot*, but her motion did not directly match the scenes that we had created for broadcast. The characters of the play were similar, but we changed the names and some of the words to create an ironic sense of our presence as exiles on Panic Radio.

ARCHIVE
The mongrels were in the kitchen
and barked at the constitution
then the sector agent up with a ladle
beat them to death
and buried the mongrels next to Beckett
at Cimetière du Montparnasse.

MOBY DICK
So, what's wrong with you?

HOLE IN THE STORM
Nothing.

MOBY DICK
Was I long asleep?

HOLE IN THE STORM
I don't know, ask the mongrels.

MOBY DICK
Where shall we go?

HOLE IN THE STORM
Not far.

SAVAGE LOVE
Oh yes, let's leave the reservation.

HOLE IN THE STORM
We can't leave the sector.

SAVAGE LOVE
Why not?

HOLE IN THE STORM
We have to come back tomorrow.

MOBY DICK

What for?

HOLE IN THE STORM

To wait for Godtwit.

MOBY DICK

He hates mongrels, and the fish are dead.

SAVAGE LOVE

Yes, and we are exiles.

MOBY DICK

So, should we wait for Bearheart?

HOLE IN THE STORM

What does he want?

MOBY DICK

Nothing.

HOLE IN THE STORM

Nothing, he wants nothing?

MOBY DICK

Who then?

SAVAGE LOVE

Samuel Beckett.

HOLE IN THE STORM

Ah! Yes, the exiled Beckett.

MOBY DICK

No better exile than Beckett

SAVAGE LOVE

Samuel Beckett waited in exile, and he waited with exiled natives for liberty, waited out the rack and ruin of reservations, and now we must wait for Beckett.

8

ARCHIVE

The White Earth Continental Congress, an association of more than three thousand native citizens, was inaugurated in the same year as the certification of the Constitution of the White Earth Nation.

The Congress has become the native source of original critical thought for twenty years, the traces of natural reason, cultural uncertainties, survivance, and without the donor politics of academic institutions.

Justice Molly Crèche and Clément Beaulieu, delegates to the constitutional conventions, proposed the White Earth Continental Congress to counter the obvious cognitive dissonance of egalitarian governance, ironic stories of native survivance, and notions of cultural victimry. The Congress celebrated more than a century of native achievements in history, newspapers, education, military service, literature, art, and athletics since the establishment of the White Earth Reservation.

The Constitution was an obvious observance of creative irony and continental liberty, and the Congress was the native count of resistance and cultural survivance in the past two centuries. The sentiments and native memories of democratic governance, the literary recognition of creative narratives, and the original scenes of cosmoprimitive art, or the actual portrayals of native motion and visionary images on rock, hides, ledger paper, and canvas, were extraordinary practices when compared to creative narratives, conceptual and expressionistic art of the modern world.

The Constitution started with new stories of totemic unions and ended with exile, but the end became another round of creation stories, once more the ironic creation of a new spirited culture was in natural motion, in the clouds, and out of the hands of sector agents.

The Canadian government recognized the theories of transmotion, or natural motion in literature and art, and praised the community voice of Panic Radio. Clearly that positive support of native expression was not the same, of course, as a formal and political recognition of the exiled Constitution of the White Earth Nation, but the sentiments provided at least a promise to negotiate the native ethos of continental liberty.

Augustus Hudon Beaulieu was the native publisher of the *Progress* and later the *Tomahawk*, the first weekly newspapers on the White Earth Reservation, nineteen years after the federal removal treaty in 1867. The editor of the *Progress,* Theodore Hudon Beaulieu, wrote critical articles about the corruption of federal agents, and the newspaper clearly anticipated the ethos of native resistance and survivance. The bold and erudite stories in these two newspapers, along with local, state, national, and international news, and advertising, clearly revealed a cosmopolitan perspective on native politics and the cultures and problems around the world. The publisher and editor were critical of federal policies but they could not have imagined the actual abrogation of the treaty and the recurrence of authoritarian endorsement sectors.

The first issue of the *Progress* was published on March 25, 1886, and the second issue of the weekly newspaper was published more than a year later on October 8, 1887, because federal agents had confiscated the newspaper and the actual rotary press, and ordered the editor and publisher to leave the reservation, the very first instance of banishment on the White Earth Reservation.

The publisher and editor accepted sanctuary at the mission church. The Benedictine priests were aware of the politics and defended the right to publish a newspaper on the reservation. The Episcopal Church, however, had endorsed the federal agents and the seizure of the *Progress*, a devious competition with the Benedictine mission for native souls and signatures.

The United States District Court ruled in favor of the constitutional right to publish a newspaper anywhere in the country. The second issue of the *Progress* reported with a literary sense of irony, "Now that we are once more at sea, fumigated and out of quarantine, and we issue from dry dock with prow and hull steel-clad tempered with truth and justice, and with our clearance registered, we once more box our compass, invite you all aboard, and we will clear port, set sails to favorable breezes, with the assurance that we will spare no pains in guiding you to a 'higher' civilization."

The eight exiles sailed on the *Baron of Patronia* more than a century later with the same sense of native resistance and survivance, and with an entirely new course to reinstate a native nation and continental liberty at Fort Saint Charles on Manidooke Minis.

The Constitution of the White Earth Nation was created with moral imagination, and the spirited preamble, rights, and principles were in natural motion everywhere, in the air with dream songs, a magical and moral flight, and the solace of the White Earth Continental Congress became a heartfelt sanctuary of native resistance and the inspiration of a new literature of exile and continental liberty.

The Congress honored William Whipple Warren, one of the first native historians. He served on the territorial legislature and published the *History of the Ojibway Nation* in 1885, two years before the first edition of the *Progress*. The Warren family moved from La Pointe, a French fur trade post on Madeline Island in Lake Superior, to Crow Wing, Minnesota, and then to the White Earth Reservation.

The Congress instituted a native thesis of original ideas, theories of resistance and survivance, philosophy, literature, and history that fully embraced the articles and principals of the Constitution of the White Earth Nation, such as totemic unions and artistic irony. That creative thesis has continued in exile, and has advanced the notion of transmotion in art and literature.

Captain Gichi Noodin navigated the *Baron of Patronia* one clear morning to Massacre Island, a ghostly place near Bay Island southeast of Oak Island in Canada. Justice Molly Crèche broadcast the solemn journey on Panic Radio. She told stories about the gruesome massacre on the island during the expansion of the fur trade more than three centuries earlier. Chewy was moved by the stories and honored with dream songs the tormented spirits on the island.

Jean Baptiste La Vérendrye, the eldest son of the Pierre Gaultier de La

Vérendrye who established the fur post at Fort Saint Charles and first traded with natives in October, 1734, and Father Jean-Pierre Aulneau, the Jesuit priest and missionary, and nineteen voyageurs of New France, were attacked and brutally murdered on Massacre Island.

No one can understand why the assassins, probably the Eastern Dakota, were so enraged by the new trade with the Cree, Assiniboine, and Anishinaabe that they beheaded the priest and voyageurs. La Vérendrye returned the heads and bodies of his son, the priest, and the voyageurs for burial at Fort Saint Charles.

Gichi Noodin anchored the *Baron of Patronia* close to the rocky shore. The exiles punted to a narrow stone landing. The trees swayed with the wind and the sound created a sense of menace. Later the wind circled the island, and the trees canted in one direction and then another. The chickens were silent on the bow, and the mongrels were shied by the spirits, the traces of rage on the island, and would not leave the houseboat.

Gichi Noodin shouted the names he could remember, Pierre, Jean Baptiste, and several times the word *voyageur, voyageur, voyageur* into stone panic holes. The other exiles searched for seams in the stone, hollows near the trees, and shouted names of the native dead, any names of the dead into panic holes. Surely the spirits of the young beheaded trader, missionary priest, and voyageurs remained in the stone of Massacre Island.

Chewy created a native dream song to honor the lost spirits on the island, and with a haunting soprano voice she sang into the trees, not the stone, not to panic holes, but into the clouds. Her voice wavered with emotion for the spirits of the voyageurs.

clouds overhead
echo my voice
your spirits
with a pleasant sound
over the island
lake of the woods
everywhere

my voice is heard
with your spirits
everywhere
everywhere in the clouds

Savage Love turned that solemn morning around with her usual critical cues about creation, last words, and death as the natural start of
stories. The end was always the start, the end of creation was the start,
not the terminal creeds, and the murder of the traders was the start of
our exile and ironic stories in the autumn gaze of liberty.

Moby Dick raised the anchor and the *Baron of Patronia* cruised back
along the international border near Fort Saint Charles on Manidooke
Minis. Sardine smiled on deck and White Favor whistled at the wake
of Massacre Island.

Savage Love was a shaman of native stories, and she got the stories
right at the start, over the cultural signatures of closure and denouement, that only ironic stories saved natives from fascist traditions and
victimry.

The stories of exile were ironic, never the stories of perfect victims.
The mongrels had nothing to bark about, there was no absence of irony
in exile, or, maybe everything was barkable in exile and the mongrels
decided to remain silent until winter. The exiles escaped the sector and
turned back the false memories, but there was no escape from the turn
of seasons at Fort Saint Charles.

Panic Radio had broadcast on several nights the open invitation to
cruise with eight exiles, five mongrels, and nine chickens for a day on Lake
of the Woods, and to honor the memory of William Hole in the Day on
Remembrance Day, Armistice Day, and Veterans Day, November 11, 2034.

Gichi Noodin was not certain that many natives would brave the cold
wind in canoes and boats to celebrate native soldiers who had served
in every continental and world war, French and Indian War, Civil War,
Spanish-American War, First World War, Second World War, Korean War,
Vietnam, Afghanistan, and the many wars in the Middle East.

William Hole in the Day had been honored every year on Remembrance Day. He was a dapper dresser, and a great shaman warrior in military uniform, a marvelous trace of the trickster stories of creation. Panic Radio broadcast several personal stories about Hole in the Day on three nights before Remembrance Day. He enlisted in the United States Navy and served in the Spanish-American War. Later he served in the North Dakota National Guard on the border of Mexico and the United States during the Mexican Revolution.

Chewy told the story that Hole in the Day enlisted in North Dakota because the Minnesota National Guard had joined federal soldiers to declare war against his relatives and other natives at Sugar Point and Bear Island on the Leech Lake Reservation in 1898. Hole in the Day would never serve with the enemies of his name and family.

Hole in the Day refused to wait for the United States to declare war against the demons of the German Empire in the First World War. He crossed the border and enlisted in the Ontario Regiment and served in the Canadian Expeditionary Forces in France.

Private Hole in the Day was wounded, poisoned by mustard gas in the Battle of Passchendaele in Belgium, and evacuated to a hospital. He died at the Canadian General Hospital in Montréal on June 4, 1919. Hole in the Day was a warrior of continental liberty.

The Libertus Flotilla, more than fifty pontoon boats, houseboats, sailboats, cabin cruisers, fishing boats, and decorated canoes, circled the *Baron of Patronia* that cold Remembrance Day on Lake of the Woods. The exiles and mongrels were on deck to salute the native flotilla.

Ronald Libertus, the portly native humanist in his late nineties, heard the invitation on Panic Radio to honor the memory of Hole in the Day and contacted his many friends around the state to join together that morning as a flotilla of liberty on Lake of the Woods. By the time the boats arrived the name Liberty Flotilla had been rightly changed to the Libertus Flotilla.

Libertus was honored with the native soldiers.

Gichi Noodin had not announced on Panic Radio that the exiles were in need of anything, but the natives in the flotilla brought huge bags of dog food, ice augers, spears, solar heated vests and mittens, chicken feed, peanut butter, chocolate, wild rice, dried beans, native pinch bean coffee, jerky, heavy socks knitted by the elders, four cases of French wine, and new spectacles for Chewy.

The Libertus Flotilla followed the *Baron of Patronia* late that afternoon to the boat dock near Fort Saint Charles. The exiles started four great fires near the shore and more than a hundred natives in the flotilla celebrated Remembrance Day, saluted William Hole in the Day, shouted out the names of other honorable native soldiers.

Hole in the Storm slowly waved his hands and danced around the fire. The motion of his painterly shadow reached over the circle of natives and created an abstract presence of the ancestors of the ancient fur trade, the heirs of continental liberty.

Savage Love moved closer and traced the shadows of Hole in the Storm. The slow gestures were natural, steady, because the two exiles had danced together many times at the Gallery of Irony Dogs. Savage Love was actually born at the gallery, a native conceived in ecstasy, and she lived out back with her mother and the irony dogs.

Hole in the Storm studied abstract art with his famous great-uncle, Dogroy Beaulieu, and created dance moves for the celebrated autumn Opéra Bouffe at the Gallery of Irony Dogs. The spirit and natural motion of that native comic opera, an ecstatic vision, had arrived by chance of exile at Fort Saint Charles.

Hole in the Day was duly honored and Remembrance Day was over, and that night around the fires the artist and devoted tutor of five irony mongrels created the ecstatic moves, visceral sways, and stray erotic gestures that were common scenes at the Opéra Bouffe. Most of the flotilla natives were inspired by the rage of the fires, waves of shadows, natural erotic motion, and danced into the night with the exiles.

Mutiny was a natural dancer, and she carried out the basic sway and motion. She circled the blaze with original paw moves, a slow step to one side, then the other, turns, a bounce, and double swish of her lacy ginger tail. Wild Rice was shy, and had never been a mongrel dancer. He was slow, and learned his moves by imitation at autumn wild rice harvests. He swayed and raised a paw, and pretended to bounce. The other mongrels trotted together behind the exiles, but their space in the circle was risky because of the fancy, ecstatic dance moves. Mother Teresa was teary, of course, and she nosed and bumped the natives in the circle of the fires. Sardine smiled and chased the shadows. White Favor turned to the side and whistled a sexy tune, and several natives whistled in return, a native tease and that was the actual start of the first comic Opéra Bouffe at Fort Saint Charles.

More natives started to whistle and dance with the exiles and mongrels, first two, then eight, ten, twenty, and within an hour most of the flotilla natives were dancing in the circle of the four fires. The shadows rebounded in natural motion, and the sound of a hand drum set the beat and nurtured the ecstatic moves of the dancers.

Waasese had prepared a laser show of native warriors and decorated soldiers in the night sky. Laser flares burst overhead, blues, reds, whites, and then native soldiers emerged in slow motion, a column of native warriors over the lake. One by one the soldiers in uniform turned to salute the natives of the Libertus Flotilla.

The seven native soldiers projected that night over Fort Saint Charles had been awarded the Medal of Honor, the highest military decoration for gallantry in actual combat. The soldiers in the night sky were seven out of more than twenty natives decorated for gallantry in the Indian Wars, World War Two, and Korea.

Chiquito, Apache scout for the United States Army, was the first laser image projected in the night sky. He was awarded the Medal of Honor for gallantry in the Arizona Territory in 1875. Some natives would never accept a scout as a decorated warrior.

Second Lieutenant Ernest Childers was Muscogee Creek, born in Broken Arrow, Oklahoma, and received the Medal of Honor for gallantry in the Second World War in Italy, 1943.

First Lieutenant Jack Montgomery was the third laser image of decorated warriors projected in a column over Fort Saint Charles. He was Cherokee, born in Long, Oklahoma, and decorated for conspicuous gallantry in the Second World War in Italy, 1944.

Sergeant Van Barfoot was Choctaw, born in Edinburg, Mississippi.

He received the Medal of Honor for gallantry in the Second World War in Italy, 1944.

Corporal Mitchell Red Cloud was Ho-Chunk, born in Hatfield, Wisconsin, and he first served in the United States Marine Corps in the Second World War in Guadalcanal and Okinawa, and received the Medal of Honor for gallantry in Korea, 1950.

Captain Raymond Harvey was Chickasaw, born in Ford City, Pennsylvania, lived in Sulphur, Oklahoma, and received the Medal of Honor for gallantry in Korea, 1951. He was also awarded the Silver Star, Bronze Star, French Croix de Guerre, and was later promoted to lieutenant colonel in the United States Army.

Master Sergeant Woodrow Keeble was Santee Dakota, Sisseton Wahpeton Oyate, from Lake Traverse Reservation in South Dakota. He served in Guadalcanal in the Second World War, and received the Medal of Honor posthumously for gallantry in Korea, 1952. He was also awarded the Silver Star, Bronze Star, and Purple Heart. Sergeant Keeble was wounded twice in World War Two and three times in Korea.

The Libertus Flotilla natives saluted the laser column of gallant native soldiers who had been awarded the Medal of Honor. White Favor whistled, almost the tune of taps on a military bugle. Mutiny swished her lacy ginger tail to honor the warriors.

Chewy moved slowly through the circle of natives to the center of the fires. She raised her hands to celebrate the new nation of exiles and announced the first performance of the White Earth Anthem. Chewy had created the anthem on the *Baron of Patronia* the first night we crossed as exiles the international border of Lake of the Woods. The spirit and sentiments of the anthem were derived from the preamble of the Constitution of the White Earth Nation. The rich melody and steady cadence of the anthem were similar to the French national anthem, "La Marseillaise."

Chewy wore her blue Treaty Shirt decorated with bright beaded flowers and, of course, with the signature conference stains. She turned slowly in the circle, and then gestured to the natives and to the night sky. She touched her heart, and in a tremulous soprano voice sang the native anthem for the first time. She was in perfect natural motion, and the mighty reach of her voice was enhanced with the muted sound of a hand drum. Mother Teresa was teary, and the mongrels waited in silence near the great soprano. The emotive tone of her voice resounded over the circle of fires at Fort Saint Charles.

native children of white earth
everywhere tonight
arise with vows of birthrights
stories of creation
native continental liberty
and declare forever
loyalty to the constitution
totemic unions
that honor the natural world
with hearts of courage
praise the warriors of the night

survivance in our stories
natural motion
survivance in our dreams
spirits of resistance
forever in the favor of liberty

fearsome shamans and warriors
we salute your gallantry
secure our liberty
and overcome the treasons
nations of greed
princely sovereignty
agents of the state
and sing our dreams
to the clouds
never shamed by creation
stones and totems
tributes of continental liberty

survivance in our stories
natural motion
survivance in our dreams
spirits of resistance
forever in the favor of liberty

native children of white earth
migrate with the seasons
the sandhill cranes
remember the courage
of native exiles
favor native stories
native reason
and continental liberty

The Libertus Flotilla natives were moved to tears and cheers and then as the fires cracked and sparked they stood and shouted out several times the name of Chewy, Chewy, Chewy. The natives chanted and praised the passion of her voice and the White Earth Anthem.

Ronald Libertus moved closer to the center of the fires, cleared his throat, and formally nominated Chewy Browne, the great-aunt of Moby Dick, as the president of the White Earth Nation.

That very night, November 11, 2034, one day after the thin crescent of the new moon, under the brilliant abstract portrayal of eternal stars and surveillance satellites, Chewy Beaulieu Browne, one of the thirteen Manidoo Singers, a sworn delegate to constitutional conventions, storier of fancy chickens, and the senior exile of continental native liberty, was elected by acclamation of the native voyageurs in the Libertus Flotilla. She was the first exiled president of the White Earth Nation at Fort Saint Charles.

The White Earth Anthem was a new story of creation in natural motion, and the spirited sounds of certain words in the anthem, liberty, clouds overhead, survivance, gallantry, and sandhill cranes, were sustained, an operatic chant in the rich and strong soprano voice. The anthem heard that night would last forever.

President Chewy Browne returned later with the exiles and mongrels to the nine chickens perched on the deck of the *Baron of Patronia*. One by one the fancy chickens spread their wings and clucked, clucked, clucked. Chewy was a magnificent creative storier, a shaman of ecstatic music, and the magical clouds of her breath lasted in the cold night air.

about the author

Gerald Vizenor is Professor Emeritus of American Studies at the University of California, Berkeley. He is a citizen of the White Earth Nation of Anishinaabe in Minnesota, and has published more than thirty books. His most recent publication is *Blue Ravens*, a historical novel about Native American Indians who served in the First World War in France. Vizenor received an American Book Award for *Griever: An American Monkey King in China*, the Western Literature Association Distinguished Achievement Award, and the Lifetime Literary Achievement Award from the Native Writer's Circle of the Americas.